Rejected Wolf

Book Two of the Moon Born Academy

Rejected Wolf: Book Two

ISBN: 9798412645834

Copy editing by Raven Quill Editing, LLC

Cover Designed by Raven Nordmann at Raven Covers

Chapter Header – canva

Disclaimer:
This book contains adult/mature situations.
This book may contain triggers: example mention of
rape or retelling of past abuse.
This book contains sexual encounters.
This book is a reverse harem.
That means the lead female does not choose between
her love interests and will have multiple sexual
partners.
Triggers involve mentioned of rape and murder.

Esmeray

A wolf growls, snapping its sharp teeth at me. Spit flies from its mouth with each snap.

My eyes widen as its snow-white eyes bore into me. I should be screaming and running away, but my body is frozen in place, and my throat is tightening with fear.

Its fur is completely black, as black as the night sky that surrounds us, but it has patches of crimson red that cover its body. The red drips onto the ground, soaking into the moss-covered ground. Is that blood?

My eyes scan the area. Where am I? A forest? This place feels familiar, but I'm unsure how. *The more time I keep my eyes off the wolf, the more it snaps its jaws for my attention. The noises echo in my head, bouncing around my already busy skull.* I can't think like this. *Anger rises inside of me until it finally bubbles up.*

"Shut up!" I snap, grabbing my hair.

Its teeth clatter shut, and a whine pulls from its throat.

"Go away. I need to get to my men!" It doesn't budge or move at all. "Go!"

Its head lowers as it slowly walks into the tree line of the forest, disappearing. I'm sure it is waiting for me to call it back, but I don't.

Panic sets in. I am alone. Where are my guys? Where is everyone? What happened? All I remember is the amount of pain I was in.

"Little moon," I hear a voice say, raspy and unfamiliar.

I twist, looking for the person who would be talking to me. There's not a single person in sight.

"Little moon, it's time to remember," she whispers.

My brows pull together as I turn around more. "Remember what?!" *My heart starts pounding against my chest.*

"Remember the first time you shifted. Remember who you truly are."

5

I jolt awake. My head spins at the sudden movement of my aching body sitting up. *If it spins anymore, I might puke.* Grabbing my head, my eyes move around the room. I am in the room that I stayed in at Stone's parents' house.

"Hey…" A deep voice makes me jolt and look over to one of the decorative chairs in the corner. Stone's large figure accompanies the small chair, making it look a little odd. He's wrapped in a small fuzzy blanket from the waist down, arms crossed to keep himself warm. He sends me a small, sad smile. The sadness reaches his icy blue eyes that remind me of everything.

The Midnight wolves, Goldie, the pain… Those… black smoking wolves. The pain that wasn't mine, but one of my pack members.

I sit up, pushing back the covers to search for my phone.

"What?" Stone asks in a voice thick with exhaustion.

"Who is hurt?"

"Esmeray…" His tone draws my attention. Although he looks like he was just sleeping, bags have formed under his eyes and stubble has formed on his face. The day the wolves attacked, he was clean shaved because I made fun of him for looking like a baby. It takes him three days to get a nice stubble like that going on. "Don't worry about them. Worry about you."

6

Rune Hunt

My throat runs dry as tears burn in my eyes. *How can he say that to me?* "How long was I out?"

His eyes watch me and after a moment, he finally speaks, "Three days."

I look around, touching my forearms. I remember the feeling of the wolf's teeth sinking into my flesh and the heated pain that radiated through my body, but my arm is healed now. "Who was hurt, Stone?"

He groans, running a hand through his messy chestnut hair. I love his hair cut. On the mornings we slept together, I'd run my hands over the shaved side.

"I'm not fragile, Stone!" I snap, even if I feel so fragile right now. My chest is aching for my pack mates. "I didn't protect my pack. I didn't protect you. I get it, but I—"

He lets out a tired sigh. "Esmeray, those wolves fucked you up... Tore through your flesh and basically tore you to shreds."

I shake my head. "No. You're lying. I was fine, besides my arm."

His thick dark brows pull together. "What do you remember?"

"One of the guys got hurt," I snap, but instantly regret it.

His face softens with a sigh. "You don't remember anything else?"

I raise my brows. *Does he not care about one of our guys getting hurt? Does he only care about what*

I remember? Why was he being like this? "No, Stone," I deadpan.

He removes the blanket, standing and moving to sit at the edge of the bed. He's shirtless with basketball shorts that hang low at his toned hips. My eyes run down the tattoos covering his broad chest, but they stop at the chiseled abs. *Not the time.* "Esmeray, when we found you, you were basically half dead... The wolves that attacked had a toxin embedded in their nails and teeth, so every time they scratched or bit you, you were infected…"

I blink. "So, am I a zombie, or—or a vampire, or something?"

He doesn't chuckle like I want him to. "They are trying to figure out what those demon wolf things are, and why their bites are infecting people. They said their bites are like nightshade poison…"

I wait for him to speak more.

"But you, Esmeray, are the only one that healed yourself. Your body fought off the poison, and that's why you are here, in my house instead of a hospital."

I look down and whisper, "Are the others dying?"

He watches me and touches my toes to comfort me. I feel like whatever he's going to say next is going to hurt. His hands are warm against my icy body. "About twenty kids were hurt in the attack. Nine have died so far."

My eyes sting. "But our pack? Are they okay?"

He lets out a sigh. "Krew has been scratched and infected."

My heart drops and tears well in my eyes. "In his shoulder?" I question, touching mine absentmindedly.

He nods.

"Is... he dead?" I spit out, scared of his answer, but I needed to know.

He shakes his head. "He's in the ICU at a hospital nearby, but it's not looking good for him."

I throw the blanket over my body, launching myself off the bed. My phone is on the nightstand, the only place I didn't look. I open my phone to see a few texts from Zeno and Kai, but none from Krew. I quickly call Krew's phone, but it goes straight to voicemail. Fear and nerves churn my stomach as my fist clenches around my phone.

"Esmeray," Stone says, rounding the bed and reaching out for me.

I slap away his hand as tears roll down my cheek. "How are you okay? Krew might die! And you're calm?!"

"Someone has to be!" he barks. I almost flinch at his tone. He blinks, chest heaving with anger. After a few deep breaths, he speaks. "I've cried enough, Esmeray."

A wave of sadness crashes into me. Although Krew might be my potential mate, he is also Stone's best friend. They have a better bond than I will ever

9

have with any of them. *I can't imagine what he's going through.* "Are you okay?" I ask in a small voice, regret filling my chest.

He let out a shaking sigh.

Grabbing his hand, I pull him into me and wrap my arms around him. He presses his cheek into mine, sighing again. "I watched you almost die and now... Krew..."

I wrap my hand around his head, nuzzling my fingers into his hair and pulling him against me. "But like me, Krew isn't going to die. Did you see him yet?"

He shakes his head.

"Let's go... together."

"You just woke up and I just..."

Fear sinks in my stomach, but it's not mine. *What's going on? Am I feeling what he feels? Is this our bond?* "Are you scared?"

He nods, eyes on the floor.

"Well, I am too... If we do this together, it won't be as scary."

"Fuck," his voice cracks. "I missed you. I was so worried."

I grab his cheek, pulling back enough to kiss his lips softly. "Yeah? Don't worry about me. I'll always be okay."

He nods, wiping some rogue tears with his palm. "I'll," he clears his throat, "call Kai and let him know we are stopping by. He hasn't left the hospital since..."

10

I shake my head. "I'll call him. Go shower and then get food for me."

He looks at me.

I touch my stomach. "What? I feel like I haven't eaten in days!"

He rolls his eyes, leaning into me. "You were tube feed. You ate."

"But I want food now!" I whine, looking up at him. "Get to work, servant."

He raises a brow, but it gets him to smile. "Krew was right about you. You are an abusive alpha."

"You guys just like toxic women," I snort but the mention of Krew makes my heart ache.

He chuckles softly and leaves my room.

My smile fades as I stare down at my phone while moving to the bathroom. Quickly, I dial Kai's number as I start the water in the shower. After two rings, he picks up. "Esmeray?" His soft voice fills me with warmth.

"Kai... Hey." I say back, unsure of what to say when he says my full name. It always makes me so nervous.

"You're awake. How are you feeling?"

I look in the mirror, seeing myself for the first time since I woke up. My dark hair is up in a messy bun, and there are bags under my brown eyes, but there's not a cut or scratch on my body. All the color has drained from my golden sepia skin, leaving it a dull fawn color. I blink, suddenly seeing blood cover

11

my whole body and pieces of my flesh hanging on muscle threads. My vitiligo patches are a pale ivory color at this point. I inhale sharply, blinking again, and I'm back to normal.

"Are you okay?" Kai asks.

"Uh." I move away from the mirror. "Yeah... I'm fine. How are you? How's Krew?"

Kai is silent before he finally speaks. "Stable. He is stable. I'm so sorry I didn't go see you when you got out of the hospital... I just wanted to be by his side and—"

I smile. "Hey, it's okay. I'd rather you be with him so he's not alone... Can I see you guys today? If you want me to. I don't want to crowd the hospital." Suddenly, I'm filled with nerves. Krew is in this mess because of me. *Those wolves were after me. My pack knows that.*

"I'd love that, baby. Text me when you are near. I'll wait for you in the lobby."

Baby... He called me baby. I let out a breath I was holding, but he can still hate me. "Hey, Kai?"

"Mhm?"

I pause, looking for the right words to say. *How do I ask if he hates me, especially during this time? That sounds selfish of me.* "I... I'll see you soon, *baby*."

"Okay. I'll see you soon," he says. I can hear his small smile, reassuring me a bit. I hang up to dial Zeno's phone. After a few rings, he picks up. "Hey."

12

His deep voice sends a shiver down my spine. "Esmeray?"

I sigh. "Yeah, it's me... How are you? Are you hurt?"

He let out a chuckle. "Are you worried about me right now?" He takes a pause, sighing. "I should have gone with you guys to protect you, Esmeray."

"Who's to say you wouldn't have gotten hurt like Krew?" I hear him sigh as I lean against the bathroom counter. "Z?"

"Mhm?"

"As Alpha, I'm ordering you not to be hard on yourself. I'm okay and that's all that matters, besides Krew right now. Somehow my body fought this thing off and I'm grateful for that, but I need you. I don't need you blaming yourself for something that couldn't have been changed, okay?"

He takes a deep breath. "Yes. I'm sorry. I just wish things went differently for us."

I remember our kiss in the forest, how we almost had sex there. I haven't known any of these men long, despite feeling like I have. I've grown so close to four of my men, but Reed.

Reed. "I reject you as an alpha, mate, and a pack member. You are nothing to me."

My chest tightens as his voice in my head, but I can't exactly remember when he said that if he did. Maybe I dreamt it.

"I need to, uh, shower. We are going to see Krew in a few."

"Okay, I'll meet you there, E."

"Okay, see you soon." I hang up. When I try to dial Reed, he rejects my call. He's the one taking it harder than anyone that I'm the alpha. *How can a girl take the place he wanted? How can she have all of these mates?*

I wonder about that, too.

I was a server who got her thrills from riding a fast motorcycle and making sarcastic jokes to make life seem good. But truth be told, I wasn't fulfilled, just worked more to distract myself from the void.

My shoulder suddenly burns. Gasping, I grab it. *Was it another one of my mates being attacked?* But it didn't feel like that. This feels like someone has pressed hot metal against my shoulder.

I bit my lip, tilting my head up to the ceiling. "Can anything just go smoothly for once, Luna?" I ask.

Luna is our moon Goddess. She provides life to us shifters. Moon Born wolves believe in her and her ways. Midnight wolves are the ones that reject her as their Goddess.

Whatever the case may be, she was not letting anything go smooth for my pack and me.

Esmeray

Kira's arms wrap around me as soon as I step down the stairs of Stone's huge house. I didn't even know she was here. "I'm so glad you're awake and okay!" she squeals, holding me tighter.

So far, Kira is the only real friend in Moon Born Academy, and she wasn't even *my* friend first. She has known all the guys since birth as their families are all in the same pack. Her red dreads are down and falling against her shoulders, complimenting her dark umber brown skin. I'm almost envious about how smooth and even toned her skin is. Her brown eyes meet mine as she speaks more.

15

She pulls back. "God! It's so bad. The academy is closed until after Halloween."

Four months. I haven't even learned anything in the short weeks I was there. I run a hand over my face, sighing. "What's gonna happen?"

"It's in the council's hands now." Silver's voice comes off to the right side of the house. He stands in the doorway of the dining room. Stone looks so much like his father. Both tall and wide, their hair the same chestnut brown, although Stone's is a little longer than his fathers. They have the same stunning, matching blue eyes. That's the first thing I noticed about Stone when we first met.

"Hello, Esmeray. I'm so glad to see you up and looking better."

I smile, moving to Silver. He wraps one of his arms around my shoulder. "I can't exactly remember who the council is again and what they do exactly," I confess. I didn't have much time to learn about the wolf shifter world before all this happened.

Stone looks up at me from the dining room table. "The council is a bunch of higher-level wolves. Think of them as the alphas of alphas. They make most of the rules and decide what happens to those who break them. Midnight wolves might get the hammer down on them by the council because of the stunt they pulled, especially killing innocent wolves."

"Aren't they always getting into trouble? I thought Midnight wolves were always bad either way."

Rune Hunt

He shakes his head, sipping his juice. "No. They choose the path they take. They have different beliefs, but most of them tend to follow the council's rules or at least stay out of trouble."

I nod. "What do you think will happen to Bellamy and the rest? Goldie was amongst them." I know I shouldn't care about Goldie, but she was my best friend for two years and then she changed so quickly. I can't remember whether she is alive or not; I only saw her briefly before she was on me. Then I remember nothing.

"Hopefully, justice," Liza, Stone's mother, says, coming in with breakfast. "They might get locked in the Estella Prison."

I smirk. "Estella Prison? Is that, like, wolfie prison for you guys? What? No chew toys for a week?"

Stone smiles lightly, looking down. "Yes. *Wolfie* prison, Esmeray."

Stupid shit tends to come out of my mouth, especially in stressful situations, but I have more questions about the council. "Hey, Silver, since you're so old, why aren't you on the council?"

Silver clenches his chest. "Jesus, Esmeray! Way to hurt my feelings."

"How old are you? Like fifty?" I continue.

He sends me a glare. "A *woman* never reveals *her* age." He chuckles and continues. "I had the opportunity to join the council, but I chose not to.

17

Brick is on the council, though. Age doesn't matter to the council, although it sounds like it."

I nod. Brick is one of Silver's Alpha friends and he seems to have his own pack and family. Both have been so welcoming, even giving me advice on how to be the best alpha I can be. I'm failing right now, so it didn't help at all.

"Come eat!" Liza orders.

Don't have to tell me twice.

I think I physically ate my weight, but it is worth it because I feel great now, I think after breakfast.

"She ate more than me!" Silver whines like a child. He reminds me so much of my father sometimes. My father loved his family—well, it was only me—and he would always joke around with me. We would tease and laugh at each other. I feel like I can always go to Silver for anything, even though we haven't known each other long.

I roll my eyes. "Let's not forget, old people just can't eat as much."

He glares. "Do you want to get kicked out, missy?"

I roll my eyes. He'd *never.*

Stone chuckles and touches my leg. "It's time to go."

"We will be behind you guys," Liza says, quickly collecting the plates.

Rune Hunt

Part of me wants to stay and help her clean up to procrastinate, but my guys need me more than ever. It's not like I don't want to see Krew, I'm simply scared of how he's going to look.

I just nod and follow Stone outside of the house. The sun is out, and I can't help but think we would be swimming right now or at least back in class. Neither would be remotely enjoyable if we did it right now.

Stone's Jeep truck roars to life. Nerves rise in my sternum when he begins pulling from the driveway to the gates. "Calm down," he says, touching my knee to stop my bouncing leg. I didn't even notice that it was bouncing. "He's going to be okay."

"I just... I don't know how I'm going to react, I guess. I haven't even seen him yet. How did you react?"

Stone let out a breath of air. "Not great, because I refused to see him. We expected him to heal faster, but the fever kept coming back."

I let out a sigh. "They *were* after me, Stone."

"Esmeray…"

"I'm just saying. I was just wondering why they keep coming after me."

"You're the first female since the goddess to be alpha. Isn't that enough?" he says, glancing at me.

I shrug. "Maybe, but I feel like there's something we are missing."

Rejected Wolf

I remember my fevered dreams. I remember Reed's rejection words and the words of the voice. *My first shift… I've never shifted.*

A burning feeling kisses my shoulder again, making me wince and grab it again. It feels like someone just stuck a hot lighter against my skin. *Why do I keep feeling this?*

"Are you okay?" he asks, looking over at me a few times.

"Just sore. I guess I was in bed too long." It isn't a lie. My body aches and feels stiff.

He nods. "Well, I never want to see you like that again."

I watch his face, and how tense his jaw and shoulders are. *It must have been hard on him.* Reaching over the gearshift, I touch his arm. "I'm sorry, baby. It must have been hard for you."

He sighs, leaning back more into the seat. "What doesn't kill you makes you stronger, right?"

I eye his face. "We can talk about how you felt more, if you'd like."

He let out a chuckle, but then he goes silent. "You have *no* idea… It felt like my world was shattered and ending. I was going to lose my best friend and my mate. I didn't want either to happen, but I felt…"

"Helpless?"

He nods, turning the corner and pulling to a hospital parking lot. "Just had to watch."

Rune Hunt

The hospital looks like some everyday hospital that "normal" people go to. It has the same eerie feeling I get when I am about to enter a hospital. They have always been creepy to me. "This doesn't look like a vet."

The joke gets a chuckle from him, and he shakes his head as he parks. I instantly see Kai's car nearby.

"Do you think we should have brought something?" I ask, rubbing my palms together as he steps out.

"I bought him flowers and stuff the other day. I'm sure it's okay."

Nerves rise in my throat as I stare at the hospital.

"Esmeray?"

My tongue wets my bottom lip and then I pull it into my mouth with my teeth. "The last time I was in a hospital... my father... died. I'm scared if I enter again... that Krew will die, too."

Stone moves to me, touching my cheeks. "You're not some bad luck charm. We all need you here."

I look up at him, sighing. *He's right. I need to be here for them.*

He bumps his hip into mine, and says, "Plus, Krew is too stubborn to die."

That makes me smile.

Rejected Wolf

Stone pulls my chin to face him before lifting it and leaning in to kiss me. I relish in his soft lips and his taste. I've missed them, even though really for me, we haven't spent any time apart. When he pulls back, he sighs heavily.

"I'll only do this for you guys," I say, grabbing his hand and pulling him to the front. As we get closer to the door, I realize I forgot to text Kai that we were close, but I see the flash of white in the crowd of people in the lobby. My heart surges and I resist the urge to run to him. Kai stands amongst Zeno and a few other students from school. I don't know their names, but I recognize them.

As if he feels my presence, his hazel eyes lock onto mine and mid conversation, he moves to me. His eyes are puffy with bags are under them eyes, making my bottom lip quiver. His hair is messy, but it normally always is. I let go of Stone's hand, only to be picked up by Kai. I wrap my arms around his neck, letting him pull me in tightly to him.

"Hey," I mutter into his neck, legs swinging. "I feel so tall."

He lets out a chuckle, that sort of sounds like a sob. *Was he crying? Fuck.*

I run my hands in his hair, feeling the softness of it. "Hey, baby... Take a deep breath. It's going to be okay." I feel his chest rattle against mine and the wetness of his tears against my neck. I lift my legs around his waist, rubbing his hair. "Deep breaths. It's okay, Kai."

After a few breaths, his chest finally steadies. With a sniff, he sets me down, and says, "Sorry." He wipes his cheek with his palm, clearing his throat.

"Don't be," I whisper, rubbing the rogue tears away from his cheeks. "Are you okay?"

He nods.

Zeno moves to me, grabbing my shoulders and pulling me into his chest. "Hey, little one." His deep voice rumbles against me. Pressing my cheek into his sternum, I wrap my arms around him. Both of us don't pull back, drinking in the moment of being so close again. He pulls back first, and when I look up, I see his dark eyes are glossy.

Rubbing his shoulder, I mutter, "Okay, I want to go see him."

Kai takes my hand this time, but I don't think he realized I'm just as nervous as him. Maybe he did, we *did* have sex and Stone says that's how you bond with someone. I can't feel what they feel though. He leads us into the elevator and pushes the button.

Stone stays close behind, rubbing my back until we get off. Some of the nurses say hello to us as we pass by.

I cease my movements when my eyes land on Krew through the ICU glass. His normal curls are matted to his clammy, pale skin. A thick tube is down his throat, helping his chest to rise and fall with deep

23

breaths. *Oh… It feels real now.* Tears rise in my eyes and a sob catch in my throat.

Calm it down. Take a deep breath and do this for your mates. Do this for Krew.

After a deep breath, I continue walking.

Kai touches my shoulder. "Yeah, it's hard to see." He opens the door for us and lets us all pile in the small room. The monitors beeps with Krew's heart rate, and the harsh alcohol smell clouds my nose.

"So—" My voice cracks, causing me to clear my throat. "Fill me in. What's the update?"

"Fever just came back. Every time they break it, it comes back," Kai says flatly. I hate seeing him like this. He looks like a mess with his messy hair and bloodshot eyes. "Other than that, the…" He clears his throat. "The poison has entered his head. If he wakes up in the next few days, it'll be a good sign, although they have no idea how he'll be."

I nod, swallowing hard. "Thank you." I move to Krew's bedside, touching his fingers softly. "Is there anything we can do for you, Kai?" I question.

I glance over my shoulder when he doesn't answer. Tears are filling his eyes. "I just… need a minute." His voice cracks and he starts to leave the room. "Please, watch him."

Someone should go after him. I look to Stone. He nods as if he read my mind, following his friend to comfort him. "He might need you too, Z."

24

Zeno looks down and nods. "Will you be okay?"

I nod. "Go comfort him. I'll look after Krew."

He nods, moving after his friends and leaving me alone with Krew. I look back at Krew, running my hand up his arm to his shoulder. His warmth fills me. Leaning in, I kiss his cheek softly. "Krew... Last time I checked, I didn't order you to die. I order you to stay alive, not just for me, for Kai... for your pack. Please fight for your pack. I ..." My eyes tear up. *Shit.*

Moving his hand to sit with him, I rub the back of his hand, eyes glued to his face. I wish he would just open his eyes and smile at me with those dimples. I reach up, pushing his hair from his damp skin. "You know, Krew, we still got those games to beat and music to share. You still haven't taught me how to play that one game. What was it called?" *I really forgot the name.* "Got to come back and tell me so I know."

I sit there for a bit, rubbing his hand until I hear light footsteps and the door opening. The smell of black tea and oranges fills the room. *Kai.* "Esmeray."

"He's doing okay. Nothing much happened." I stand, setting his hand down on the bed before twisting around. Outside the ICU are some guys in some fancy ass suits standing with Stone and Zeno. "Who are they?"

"The council. They want to speak to us."

Esmeray

I've heard of the council exactly one time before today. Today would be the second and third. They are the highest level of wolves, and men with so much power it radiates as soon as I step into the room.

Do I bow? Do I shake their hands or am I not worthy of that? Are they royalty? I guess in the shifter world they are if everyone knows them.

Besides me.

Two gentlemen with a moon crest on their suit jackets stand with my mates, and now Reed.

"Esmeray, my name is Michael Richly," an older gentleman says, holding out his hand.

I take his hand and shake it.

"And I am Robert Tilbury," the other says, and I shake his hand too.

"Esmeray, but I guess you all knew that," I say flatly.

Michael nods. "We just have a few questions for you and your pack, if you'd like to go into a separate room for moment."

I glance over my shoulder at Krew. Kai is the first to speak up. "I'm not leaving my brother alone."

They pay no mind to Kai, looking at me to answer. "Did you not hear him?" I ask, brows pulling together. "We are not leaving my pack member alone. We can talk in his room, if you really want privacy."

Michael blinks at me, but nods.

So, I lead the way back into Krew's room. It's silent as Stone closes the door behind us. I look up at the council members, waiting for them to speak. "Ms. Devine, are you well aware of who led the attack on Moon Born?"

"I think. I've seen one of them before in South Carolina."

He nods. "So, do you know what exactly he was after?"

I blink. "I'm guessing... me?"

"Why you out of all people?"

I shrug. "I'm wondering the same thing."

Robert and he share a glance, before Robert talks. "Is Stone actually your mate?"

Rejected Wolf

I feel like I'm being questioned by the police, but I nod.

"But there's more, isn't there? Your classmates reported that you might have five mates? Do you think that's normal for a shifter?"

My eyes move to Stone. His jaw tightens and his blue eyes darken. I can almost feel his anger as I speak, "Is it even normal for there to be a female alpha? Do you have any information on how to help Krew?"

Michael lets out a snarl, making me train my eyes on him. "How come you are *healed* while all the other students haven't yet?"

"How am I supposed to know that? I just woke up and you guys are not giving me any information."

"These questions," Kai starts, "seem very unnecessary. Shouldn't you guys be figuring out how to heal the students? Maybe Esme has different blood components that can save the others."

Robert shrugs. "I'm not a researcher. That's for the doctors and nurses to manage."

My brows pull together. *Then why ask medical questions?*

Robert pulls out his phone and begins swiping at something. He flips the phone to show me a picture of myself. I'm lying in a hospital bed with a deep gash on my face showing the white flesh below. My shoulders and arms are covered with bruises and teeth marks and claw marks. "This was you two hours before you fully healed. How do you explain that?"

My stomach churn, swallowing spit to stop myself from vomiting. I barely recognize myself. "I don't know. Different wolves?"

He put away his phone. "Every single wolf we found had toxins like nightshade in their nails and teeth and you are saying different wolves attacked you?"

"I don't *know* what is going on." I throw my hands up in defense.

Michael nods. "Once Krew is dead, you will all be called in for a council meeting where—"

Anger rises in my throat like acid. "Excuse me? Krew isn't going to die."

He raises a brow at me, staring hard as if I'm going to back down. "If his fever doesn't go away, it's going to leave damage. I'm sure he'd rather be dead than a vegetable."

"We are done here," Stone interjects as my chest starts heaving. "If you have any more questions, contact Silver Wilson, but not us. Thank you. Goodbye."

Again, they both look at me, waiting for the alpha to speak, so I do. "You heard him. He was nicer about it than I would have been." They eye me for a moment. "Get out!" I stare at them until they finally leave.

Rejected Wolf

"It's going to be even worse during the actual meeting they want to have with us," Zeno says with a sigh.

I let out a breath, looking at Krew. *Of course, they thought I know something about this. Those wolves were after me.*

Arms wrap around me, and I know it's Zeno from his scent and his warmth. He rests his chin on my head, having to lean over a bit. "I hate to tell you guys this, but Krew isn't going to die," I mutter.

"Why?" Zeno questions.

"Because he's too big headed for all the poison to travel around." I mutter.

It's silent for a moment before Kai throws his head back and laughs, "Fucking idiot is too stupid to die. I doubt he would know how to, even if you gave him fucking instructions."

"Have you seen him trying to use the microwave?" Stone says, laughing.

I cackle, "Yes! Oh my god!"

Kai touches Krew's arm, smile fading after a moment. "Could you imagine a world without Krew?"

I shake my head. "Don't even want to. He'll be okay, so we won't have to picture it."

Kai let out a sigh. "Those council members—"

"Are old shriveled up dicks," I snap, twisting to look up at him. I let out a sigh before running my hand over his chest. His hazel eyes are very red, and bags

30

are forming under his eyes. "You look exhausted. When's the last time you ate or slept?"

He blinks down at me. "I don't even know."

"Stone, stay with Krew. Zeno and Reed, will you go to get food for him? I'll text you where Kai settles down."

Reed and I share a look, the first since he entered the room with the elders. His jaw tightens and his eyes move away. But he leaves with Zeno to get Kai food.

"Esmeray," Kai protests.

"Follow me. Come on. You can use a shower and a nap."

"I... I can't leave him, Esmeray. What if something happens?"

I grab his face and pull it to me. "It's an order. You can't do anything stressed and tired. We will get you as soon as he opens his eyes, okay? We have your back and his. Trust us."

He nods, sighing. "Okay..." I grab his hand, pulling him away from his brother, which I feel bad about, but I know he needs it.

At the first sight of the nurse, I ask her about any rooms for families to sleep in. She points us to a hall of separate rooms. I text Zeno the room number and where to find Kai. Luckily, there's a twin size bed and a small bathroom that he can shower in with a few towels and scrubs.

31

"Take a shower. Zeno and Reed are going to come back soon. I'll be with Krew."

He grabs my hand and pulls me back before I can leave. "Esme. Can you stay with me? I can't be alone."

I scan his face before nodding "I'll be right here. Go shower." I sit alone on the bed, texting Stone as Kai showers.

Me*:* I'm going to stay with Kai. He doesn't want to be alone. Will you call one of us as soon as anything changes?

Stone: Yes. Text me if you guys need anything.

As soon as Kai gets out of the shower, Reed arrives with the food. He doesn't say anything when he sees me. It's not the right time to call me a whore, apparently. As soon as Kai is finished eating, he lays down shirtless. "Can you lay down with me?" he asks.

I kick off my shoes, and smile. "On this small ass bed?"

He nods, scooting over toward the wall. Shrugging off my light jacket, I climb into the bed with him, putting my leg over his and resting my head on his chest. "Can I have a kiss?"

"Kai, you don't have to ask for one." Snorting, I twist and turn my head upward. My fingers run up his neck, touching his sharp jaw and nuzzle them into his damp hair. I lean in, kissing his pink lips softly.

Rune Hunt

He reaches up, pulling my lips into his hard. Our kiss is passionate and full of heat and lust, lips moving with each other. When our tongues finally touch, I groan. He grasps my hair, pushing his weight on top of me.

"Kai, we shouldn't," I say breathlessly.

He ignores me, peppering kisses against my neck and shoulder.

"Kai, you are going through shit and—"

He grabs my neck harshly and snaps, "So, shut up and make me forget."

I shudder at his touch. Need fills me, making me spread my legs further for him. "Are you sure about this?"

"I have been trapped in my head these last few days. I almost lost my mate… I'm about to lose my brother."

"Kai, don't say that."

His voice cracks as he continues. "For a moment, I just don't want to feel anything or think about anything. I want to just feel you." He grinds his hips right into my core. "I've missed you." His hands run up my sides, brushing against my bralette, instantly moving it to the side to grasp my heavy breasts. My nipples harden under his touch and I thrust my hips out to rub against his hard length. I gasp, grabbing his shoulder.

"Are you sure?"

Rejected Wolf

Heat is swirling in my stomach when his eyes meet mine. "Yes, Esme."

Pushing him back onto his knees, I slide my shirt over my body. He takes off my bra next, letting them both fall to the ground.

He grunts, reaching down and running his tongue over my nipple. I grasp his hair, moaning softly. *We are still in the hospital. I can't be loud.*

But when his hand dips into my pants and cups my sex, I throw my head into the pillow, trying hard not to moan loudly. Slowly, his long fingers find my clit, circling it until I'm writhing under him.

"Fuck, Esme. Hearing you moan is so beautiful," he mutters as his fingers move faster.

I grab his wrist, trying to push him back from doing that to me, even though I don't want him to stop. I'm panting, unable to breathe. It feels like it's been forever since his last touched me. My legs are shaking, and my breath is staggering. I close my eyes, swallowing hard. I didn't want to come so quickly, but I can't help it. "K—Kai. I'm— I'm—"

"Come for me. Come for me, baby."

I listen, pressing my head into the pillow and biting my lip to stop myself from crying out. I squeeze my eyes shut, digging my nails into his arm, coming undone for him. It leaves me breathing hard and in cloud nine.

"Good girl," he mutters, slowing down and pecking my chin and neck. "Are you ready for me?"

34

"I don't know, am I?" I ask in a teasing tone

His middle finger dips low into my folds, feeling my dripping juices. "*Jesus*." My body is always ready for him.

I wrap my arms around him, pulling him close. "Fuck me, Kai. Please."

He takes off his own pants as I quickly take off mine. I glance down, licking my lips at his size. Pulling the blanket over us, he settles between my legs. I look up at him, resisting to ask him if he's sure about this. But he grips his dick between us and guides the swollen tip through my folds.

I gasp, feeling his long length stretch me to the fullest. It feels like forever before he's fully inside of me, and once he is, we both share a moan. "Fuck," I gasp.

He smiles, kissing me for a moment. Fisting his soft hair, I pull him close as I run my thighs over his. He pulls back, thrusting back into me. Kai takes his time with me, fucking me so slow, but deep. It feels intimate for me, something I've never really had. Stone and I are always so fast paced and rough.

I grip his shoulder, digging my nails into his skin. "Oh fuck, Kai." I roll my hips to meet with him. It pushes him to go deeper. He closes his eyes, moaning. I pull him close, pressing my breasts into his sweating chest. He rocks his hips hard, running his hands over the sides of my breasts before gripping my hips. He drives in deeper, making me shove my face into his shoulder. "Don't stop."

His fingers dig into thighs, clenching me. "Why would I, baby?"

The tightness builds in my hips. "I'm getting close. Please."

He pounds into me hard, cursing into my neck.

Finally, the tightness is too much that I arch into him, throwing my head back. "I'm coming, Kai! Kai!" I shout in a whispered tone.

He picks up speed, driving himself harder into me. It throws me over the edge. I grip his shoulders, trying to hold back my cries. He rides my high, biting my shoulder as he slowly thrusts himself deeper into me.

"Fuck, I'm coming." He pulls out.

I grab his wet dick, jerking him off slowly yet deeply. He drops his head, hair fanning out from his sweaty forehead. And when he comes, he lets out a low groan, hips thrusting with my hand while his cum sprays all over my chest.

Esmeray

Sadly, we don't wake up to my phone ringing, meaning Krew still isn't awake. Kai shifts first and sits up, waking me up. He rubs his head, groaning. "What time is it?"

I check my phone seeing it's almost midnight at this point. We slept the entire day together, yet I woke up with a pounding headache. "A bit after eleven."

Kai rolls my body, kissing my chest before standing and getting dressed. "Thank you," he mutters.

Rejected Wolf

I smile, feeling the hot heat touching my shoulder again. Inhaling sharply, I slowly smooth down my frizzy hair. "Do you feel refreshed?"

Nodding and grabbing my hand, we walk back to Krew's room. Like expected, he's still out, but Stone is up, leaning on the bed and watching television. I smile at him.

Stone stands, stretching. "Fever is there, but lower. That's it."

Kai nods, hugging him. "Thank you. Go get some rest."

Stone sighs, nodding.

"I can stay," I offer.

Kai shakes his head. "Take Stone home. He's probably too tired to drive."

I nod, moving to him. He stands, just to pull me into his chest. "Call me if anything changes, Kai."

He nods, kissing my lips quickly before sitting. I hold onto Krew's hand for a moment before Stone and I walk out.

"Sorry we were sleeping for a while," I apologize as we get to the parking lot and almost back to the Jeep.

Stone squeezes my hand. "Don't worry about it. He needed you."

I nod.

He pulls me to him. "Don't crash the car or I'll have your ass."

"Oh! I might crash then," I tease.

He smacks my ass, grumbling at me, but opens the driver's side for me.

I hop into the Jeep, realizing how tiny I really am as I have to adjust the seat a bunch of times. Stone chuckles at me when he slides into the passage seat. "Shut it, you jolly green giant."

Most of the ride home is quiet. It made me realize I haven't been behind the wheel in a while. It's weird to me, especially when driving and riding my motorcycle was my comfort thing to do. *Now it was a different type of riding.*

My shoulder burns as we get further down a dark road with trees surrounding it. It's pretty dark, but at least I know where I'm going. But the further we get into the road, the more my shoulder burns. Flames seem to embed themself into my shoulder, burning hotter than before, making me groan.

Something dark jumps out in front of the Jeep and I slam on the breaks. "Fuck!"

Stone grabs the dashboard and then places his arm over my chest to stop us from slamming forward.

Dark eyes peer up at me over the hood of the Jeep. Its white fur matted with sweat and dirt. "Wolf. Shifter?" I asks breathlessly.

Help, a voice says.

A burst of white pain runs through my shoulder at the voice. I gasp, grabbing my shoulder while not removing my eyes from the wolf.

Keep going, brother.

39

Rejected Wolf

I jerk my head to the side, seeing a dark-haired wolf stepping from the shadows.

"Another? Do you think they are from Midnight?" Stone asks.

She can hear us.

My eyes drift to the one in front of the Jeep.

No, she can't, the other says. *Go before they kill us like those Oni ones tried to do.*

"Oni?" My shoulder blazes as they both take off into the other side of the woods. Finally, I throw open the door, shouting, "Wait! I can help!"

But they are already gone.

"What?" Stone asks. "Get in the car before more comes."

"He was hurt, Stone!" I say, sitting back down and huffing. "He wanted help."

"How did you know that?"

My brows pull together. "Didn't you hear them? The one asked for help and the other said we'd hurt him. We have to go after them, Stone."

He touches my cheek. "Esmeray, wolves can't hear each other. Maybe you're tired and thought that was what was going on."

"But... But…" *I've heard him before in his wolf form. He didn't know that?* I swallow as my body sags. *Maybe he's right. I heard what I wanted to hear. Maybe I wanted them to be hurt, so I can actually help someone.* I nod, finally before driving back to his house.

Rune Hunt

Stone falls asleep as soon as his head hits the pillow, laying on his bare stomach. Although I'm still exhausted and drained, I sit there staring at the beautiful ceilings. The Wilson's couldn't have picked a better pattern, to be honest. The tiled ceiling is amazing matte black and swirled with gold.

I blink. *Okay, I do need slee*p.

Ring! Ring!

I jolt awake, not even remembering falling asleep. My phone rings and vibrates on the nightstand and I answer it.

"Hello?" I say in a hoarse, tired voice. Stone shifts away from me.

"He's awake," Kai's sweet voice says from the other side. It takes me a tired second to jolt out of bed.

"Krew?!" I saw with a gasp.

That gets Stone to look up.

"Yes! Fever died overnight and he woke up a few minutes ago. He's asking for you all."

I almost didn't believe him until I hear Krew's voice in the background. "Tell her to bring my video games. I'm gonna get bored in here."

"We will be right there." I hang up, staring at Stone.

"What? What's going on?" Stone sits up, groaning.

I break out in a smile, laughing with relief. Tears threaten to run down my cheek. Stone smiles instantly rushing at me and scooping me into his arms, feeling my excitement.

"He's awake?" he asks with cheer in his voice.

"Yes! He's awake!" We hug each other, laughing before I slap his shoulder. "Get dressed! Come on!"

Seeing Krew's face smiling and seeing him standing makes me stop in the middle of the hall. Stone keeps going, but I needed a second because my eyes are tearing up again.

I came here and he didn't die. I watch him hug Stone, laughing about something. I bit my bottom lip to stop it from quivering.

He smiles, showing off that dimple that makes my knees weak and my stomach have butterflies. Last time we rarely talked, he screamed at me. *For what? I can barely remember it.*

His hazel brown eyes find mine through the glass. A small smile runs across his face.

☐I☐ guess it's time to go inside. I☐ move to the room and before I can say anything, his arms wrap around my shoulders. I'm taken back for a second before wrapping my arms around his waist.

"Thought you died," he mutters in my hair.

☐I☐ pull back. "Me?! You fucking— You just almost died!" ☐I☐ hit his arm. "Don't be stupid again, idiot."

Rune Hunt

"Abusive, Alpha!" Krew howls, poking my sides. □I□ let out a giggle, pushing him lightly. "I'm serious. I'm glad we are all okay. But I do need food and games."

I roll my eyes, lifting the bag of his video games. He basically sobs at the sight.

"Did your parents come see you?" Zeno asks with a chuckle.

"They are on their way. But I know they were here yesterday," Krew says, sitting back on the bed and throwing his hands behind his head. "You want to know how I know?"

I raise a brow, looking at the others.

"I could still hear," he says, meeting my eyes,

He heard me begging for him to come back? I try not to show that I know what he meant, and say, "So you heard us talking shit about you?"

He smiles. "Yeah. Something like that. Food?"

Reed says with a nod, "On it."

"I want coffee too. The good kind."

Reed sends him a look, making me take him in. He seems to be upset about something. His dark brown hair hangs down to his forehead. His dark brows are pulled together, but there's a small smirk on his pink lips. Tattoos cover most of his body, especially the one that crosses his neck, saying "killing me softly." "You're lucky you almost died."

I smile, but when Reed looks at me, it fades. There are no emotions in his gaze as he turns and

43

leaves with Zeno. Zeno at least waves bye to me. I want to spend more time with him for sure. Our almost-sex in the woods makes my stomach stir.

I glance at Stone, who is setting up the gaming system for Krew. He doesn't seem to be worried about the wolves yesterday, or he at least doesn't want to destroy the moment for the twins. Honestly, it's not important, but I can't stop thinking about them. Pressure rises in my face as I can tell I'm getting a headache, and my body aches like sleep is needed, but I slept a lot the last couple of days.

Maybe it's the bright ass lights in the hospital.

"Are you okay?" Krew asks.

I look up, not realizing I'm touching my head. "Huh? Oh, uh, tried. Barely slept last night."

Out of the corner of my eyes, I see Stone and Kai share a look.

Krew scoots back, holding the remote. "You can sleep on me."

"No, I'm okay." *How weird would that be? Today isn't about me.*

Kai sighs. "Esmeray, if you're tired, you can sleep in the bed. I'm sure Krew won't be sleeping anytime soon with how much sleep he's gotten. Better than going all the way home."

"She has to sleep with me, okay? Not without me," Krew says, wiggling his brows.

I let out a sigh, making my head pound hard. "No, I want to spend time with you guys."

Krew shrugs, eyes on the screen. "Twenty bucks, you fall asleep in that chair and then wake up complaining about your back."

I roll my eyes. *Maybe I need a coffee too, but I hate coffee.* I only drank it on busy days at the diner. Pulling out my phone, I text Zeno.

Me: Hey, handsome. Can I have hot chocolate?

It takes him a second to text me back. The guys are already screaming at the television and the game on it.

Zeno: Do you only call me handsome when you want something?

Me: No, I'd call you, Daddy.

I send it without thinking and instantly regret it. I've only called Stone, Daddy.

Zeno: No. No. Papi.

My cheeks heat up.

Me: Sorry. Hey, Papi chulo. ¿Me puedes traer un chocolate caliente?

Zeno: ¿Crema batida?

My mouth waters at the thought of his deep voice whispering "whipped cream" in my ear. Zeno is ten times hotter when he speaks Spanish.

Me: Please. Por favor.

Zeno: Got you, beautiful.

But I didn't want the conversation to end.

Me: Are you texting and driving?

Zeno: No, I'd never do that. Reed is driving.

45

Rejected Wolf

Me: Don't let him spit in my drink, please. I mean, I like that, but not from him.

Zeno sends laughing emojis.

Zeno: Can I spit in it, mami?

My pussy throbs and my lips part.

Me: Added flavor. Also call me mami in real life and we will finish what we started back in the woods.

He sends a winking emoji.

Zeno: We will see if you're brave enough.

"Who are you flirting with?" Krew says, trying to lean over and see my phone.

I snatch my phone away. "Your mom."

"I don't know why you'd want to flirt with that old lady, but have fun."

I roll my eyes, looking up at him.

"You know, Esme, my back hurts so bad." He groans dramatically.

I sent him a glare. "So, you have a twin for a reason."

Kai snorts. "I'm not rubbing his back."

Krew pushes his bottom lip out at me. "Please. Come rub my back. I almost died." He moves forward. I let out a sigh, kicking off my shoes and crawling on the bed. I'm careful to not hurt him more as he settles between my thighs. I get to work rubbing his back, trying not to focus on my pounding headache.

Krew groans. "Yeah, that's the spot!"

Rune Hunt

I can't help but smile. He's lucky he almost died.

Krew

Luckily, my hospital gown hides the boner I have growing. *How dare Esmeray be this hot and how dare she hug me like that before?* She doesn't even look like she is dying. Her curls have the same shine and bounce as before. Her skin is still the even tan it was. She's so short; she had pressed her head into my sternum. Even now, her legs barely round my waist.

I try to focus on the game in front of me, but it's hard when her crotch is pressed against my butt and her hands are running up and down my back.

The urge and need to fuck her is so much higher. I can tell it is for Zeno too, but he doesn't show it.

She almost died. Our mate almost died.

She looked like Carrie from that one horror movie, *Carrie*, when she came out the forest after the fight at Moon Born had died down. When I rushed to her, I saw her eyes were pure white, and when she passed out in my arms, I swear her heart stopped. I didn't care about me or my wound, only worried about her.

I genuinely believe Esmeray talking to my ear while I was in the coma made it so much easier to recover, like she was my guardian angel.

When it's Kai's turn to play with Stone, I lean into her, letting her rest her hands. I didn't even need a backrub, but the sensation of being close to her makes me feel better.

She rests her hands on my lower back, looking up at the television and commenting on how shit we are. Yet if she played, we'd truly see how shit she is. I grab her toes, softly rubbing them. I ignore her stiffening.

I need to touch her, even if it is just her toes.

It does take a while for Zeno and Reed to come back with food, and I trap Esmeray from moving away from me, despite the looks Reed send us.

He's missing out.

49

Rejected Wolf

Zeno hands her a drink whispering in her ear, something like, "Here you go, mami."

I smirk, feeling her hips dig into my back. *I smell her...* I always smell something sweet when she is turned on, and it's often. She doesn't know that we—as mates—can smell that but I wasn't going to tell her anything.

She eats her donut and drinks her drink, dancing to invincible music. I notice she does that when she eats or drinks anything good. It makes me smile as I eat the breakfast sandwich they got me. He got the others stuff too. Zeno is always so nice; he thinks of others all the time.

Esmeray owes me twenty dollars because after about twenty minutes, she passes out right against my back, snoring into my shoulder. Her hands rest at my waist, legs around me.

"What has gotten her so tired?" Zeno questions, adjusting the blanket so she's covered.

"Wouldn't be surprised if she is pregnant and doesn't know whose it is," Reed mumbles.

My jaw tightens as a rush of anger swirls through me. "We have let you get away with saying shit," I start. "It's getting to the point that it's pissing me off when you breathe. Knock it off before I hurt you again."

Reed snorts, looking to the others for help. But none of the others come to his rescue. "She's playing

you guys. How could she not know she's a shifter?
Have no family or money? She's lying."

"I know you had your daddy," Stone starts,
voice low. "But in the real world, people have jobs and
live paycheck to paycheck. Not everyone is as
fortunate as us, Reed. And I really doubt she cares
about money."

"She's playing you guys. I'll be here and laugh
when it becomes known."

I roll my eyes. "Whatever, *dick*. How pissed
are you that you didn't fuck her first? That Stone
became the Alpha Mate first?"

Reed's dark eyes hone in on me. I smell the
start of a shift in the air. It smells like sulfur and rain
before the storm. I don't back down. If he wants to
shift and fight, we can. This is the only time he'd
actually win, but I still wouldn't go down without a
fight.

"Calm it down," Stone orders, and although we
don't have to listen to him, Reed stands.

"It's pretty clear that all of you would rather get
your dicks wet over being my friend."

I roll my eyes. "I almost died, and you are
leaving."

"Yes, I am. Because I'm not going to around be
the reason you almost died, and yet, you have her all
over your back as if you weren't going to fuck that
other girl at the party."

"Because of you!" I snap.

Rejected Wolf

Esmeray stirs on my back, silencing us until she settles again. She's a heavy sleeper.

"You got into my head." I send a glare.

"And mine," Zeno mutters.

"You're not acting like a pack member, Reed," Kai adds.

"So, grow a pair and reject me," Reed suggests. And although I'm close to it, we'd never do that. We grew up thinking that this was our family, our pack, and we knew nothing could tear us apart, but Reed is distancing himself as if Esmeray is doing it. "Thought so." He chuckles, walking out of the room.

"He's more of an ass than he's ever been," Kai mutters.

I nod.

"She could be getting her period…" Zeno adds. I raise a brow, a little confused. "That could be why she's so tired lately."

I nod, but it doesn't *smell* like it. Especially if Stone hasn't noticed because his senses are way stronger than mine. "Do you think she's pregnant?" I can't help but ask them and to look at my twin. "Do you not know how to use the 'pull out' method?"

Kai sends me a glare. "We had sex twice and each time I didn't come in her or near her…" His face starts blazing. He's embarrassed. *Poor guy.*

"Twice?" I question. I only remember the one… time… *When did he have time to sleep with her again?* Then I gasp. "Did you fuck her when I was about to die?!"

"No!" His cheeks are bright red now, like a tomato.

I let out a laugh. "You asshole!"

Kai keeps trying to deny it and thinks I'm mad, but I'm far from it. Kai rarely fucks anyone, so this is new and kind of funny.

Ring!

Stone's phone rings and he picks it up, "Hello? Yeah, give me a second."

He stands, moving to us. I half expected him to hand the phone over to me. But instead, he shakes Esmeray awake. She stirs, and I feel her head tilt up to him.

"It's my dad."

"For me?" she questions before taking the phone.

Esmeray

"Krew is awake?" Silver questions as soon as Stone hands over the phone.

I rub the sleep from my stinging eyes before saying, "Yes."

"The council members want to schedule a meeting with you all."

53

Rejected Wolf

Taking a deep breath, I try to calm my raging headache. "He just woke up."

"They work quickly," he says.

I let out a sigh. "When?"

"Tomorrow at three. Look nice and have the whole pack there."

I glance around the room. All eyes are on me, but one pair is missing. "Yeah, we will be."

"Okay. We will be there for support. Don't worry, kiddo. We've all been through it before."

I smile, but for some reason I doubt he's been through what I've been through. The academy closed because of me. I am the first female alpha and have a guy in my pack who hates me. "Thanks. We will see you later."

He hangs up and I hand the phone back to Stone. "What's going on?" he asks.

I lean back, touching my temple. "Council meeting is tomorrow at three. Dress nice and be there on time." They all seem to agree. "Someone text Reed and tell him, unless he's coming back." He doesn't answer me when I text him. He was here when I fell asleep, though.

Krew shrugs. "He just left, so I don't think so."

My eyes narrow. "What happened?"

"Why do you think something happened?" He returns his focus to the television.

I raise a brow. "Just a gut feeling. Stone, text Reed for me." I yawn, stretching. Stone nods. "When did they say Krew can get out of the hospital?"

"They want to keep me for another night," Krew answers. "Just to make sure I'm healing correctly.

I nod.

"Why? Do you have more important things to do?"

"Yes. Yes, I do."

He glances back at me, smirking and shaking his head. Once Krew's parents come, I slips from behind him and sit next to Stone.

"Are you okay?" Stone whispers to me.

"I think stress is getting to me finally," I say, leaning my head into his shoulder.

"Do you have a headache again?" He wraps his arm around me and rubs my shoulder.

I nod.

"Do you want me to take you home?"

I shake my head. "I can endure it for Krew."

Stone nods, reaching up and rubbing my temple with two fingers. It helps the pressure a bit, and it feels so good, I don't want him to stop. "What's stressing you out?"

The meeting. Reed. My burning shoulder. My aching chest. The first time I shifted. Krew's health. Those wolves. "Nothing much." I shrug, watching

Krew's mom kiss his head. He tries to pull away, scrunching his face up in disgust. I smile.

It still amazes me that these five strangers who came into my diner ended up being the guys I want to spend my life with, and my protectors. I didn't think after the cliff that I'd ever see them again. They seem to make me smile no matter what and even then, their energy was amazing. I was attracted to them instantly, even Reed. Now, Reed's attraction is dying down between all the name calling and pissing off his pack.

"I can't believe you kids went through that," Krew's and Kai's mother, Donna, says. "How are your mental states?"

I bite back a laugh.

"Amazing," Kai starts sarcastically.

"Peachy," Zeno says, making me laugh.

Simultaneously we all say stuff like "fine" or "fantastic." We all burst out laughing.

"I think we will be fine," I say finally. "We are just grateful Krew is at least a bit normal again."

"A bit normal?" Krew scoffs. "I'm all the way normal."

"Was he even normal to begin with?" Kai questions, making me laugh. It makes me happy to know he's back to being happy.

"No, he wasn't," I add.

Krew throws a pillow at my head, making me giggle and fix my hair.

Rune Hunt

We stay in the hospital for hours until Stone suggests we leave for food. I almost forget about eating, which is a shock for me. I've been focused on Krew all day and the updates from the nurses, I forgot about myself. My headache doesn't go away, but it is a bit better from the medicine that Donna gave me.

Zeno bumps me as we all walk out together. "What are you guys going to do tonight?"

I look up at Stone, wondering if had anything in store for us. "Pizza?"

My lips curl into a smile. "The greasiest kind."

Zeno rubs his stomach. "Lucky."

"Do you want to come over?" I ask, touching his hand.

He doesn't pull away, but he says, "Mom's cooking today and she gets pissed if I don't eat what she makes."

I nod. I'm the same way, so I can't blame her.

Zeno grabs my hands, pulling me against him in a swoosh of air. His hand cradles the nape of my neck as he presses his lips into mine, harshly taking what he wants. I barely have time to react before he pulls back and then kisses my forehead. "Feel better. Text me."

Panting, I stare up at him, feeling the heat of lust pool low in my stomach. His hair is up and pulled back today, showing off his square jaw and tan, even skin. Strands of black waves from his hair frame his cheeks. His bushy brows are pulled together a bit,

57

making him look madder than he actually is. I reach up and touch the stubble of hair that is growing against his jaw, then drop it to his neck, then shoulder. *How dare he be this hot?* "Mhm…" For a moment, my headache and aching have completely disappeared.

He gives Stone a smirk before walking to his car. I can't help but look at his round ass in the black jeans he's wearing. "This should be illegal," I mutter to myself.

Stone laughs, opening the door for me.

Esmeray

Stone sets the pizza on the bed. There's nothing better than sitting in bed while eating and watching a movie.

"I need to shower before we eat," I say, kicking off my shoes.

Stone takes off his shirt, making my eyes go straight to his stomach that's riddled with abs. *Once again, this should be illegal...* A chuckle makes me look back up to his face. "Do you want me to join?"

I reach down, grabbing the hem of my t-shirt and sliding it over my head. His eyes move to my lacy black bra. I reach behind my back and unclip it, letting it fall.

59

Rejected Wolf

A smirk curls on his lips. "Damn."

"What? Do *you* want to join me?"

He nods.

I unbutton my pants and his eyes follow as I slide it over my ass and shimmy out of it. "And if I don't let you?"

He scoffs, unbuttoning his jeans and dropping them and his boxers. My eyes explore his deep V straight to his standing, hard dick.

"Dear god," I mutter.

He moves to me, fisting his cock right in front of me. "Let me join you, baby."

I kiss his lips, pulling on his shoulders. He gets the drift, lifting me and letting me wrap my legs around his hips as our lips devour each other. Heat pools in my stomach as I run my fingers into his short hair.

He guides us easily into the bathroom and sets me on the counter. His hands run down my sides before fingering my lacy panties at my hip. "Let me…" he mutters between kissing me, and I nod. *I want him to take them off.* "Rip these off."

I pull back. "Wait!"

It's already too late. The lace bites into my flesh as he pulls and rips it apart. He throws it over his shoulder as if he didn't pay a lot of money for that.

"Stone! I don't have a lot of clothing here!"

Ignoring me, he rubs his swollen tip against my soaking folds. It makes me twitch when he touches my

60

clit. "Fuck, I need you so bad," he mutters, letting his fingers brush my lips and clit more.

I moan out, thrusting my hips upward against his abs.

Stone's large hand engulfs my breast, rubbing it.

I reach between us, grasping his twitching dick and earning a long groan from his lips. I feel the sticky precum on his tip and rub it down his length. "Damn... Do you want me that bad?"

His icy blue eyes land on my eyes as he leans onto the counter. "I almost lost you."

I freeze, looking up at him. "Were you upset?"

He looks down at me. "Very. I missed you more than I've ever missed anyone in my life."

I swallow, feeling my throat drying up.

He ignores me in my sappy moment before fisting his cock and lining it up. Slowly, he enters me. I let out a sharp gasp as he stretches me. Once he's fully in, I take a deep breath and grip his shoulders. Stone is big, evident from his large body as well.

"Open your eyes. I want to watch your face while I fuck you." His palm grasps my cheek and I let my eyes flutter open. He smiles at me. "Are you okay, baby?"

"We've had sex a lot and I still can never get used to your size." I roll my hips, trying to make the pain go away.

Rejected Wolf

He chuckles, adjusting my ass so I'm on the edge of the counter. He inhales sharply, standing straight. "Fuck, you look so beautiful around my cock."

My pussy throbs around him. "Jesus! Are you going to fuck me or stand there looking pretty?"

His abs flex and shoulders roll. "Just taking in the moment." He suddenly grabs my hair roughly, tilting my head back to look up at him. "If you died, we'd never be able to do this again." His hips dip low as he pulls out, slowly. Then he slams himself into me. My mouth opens with a small noise, unable to pry my eyes away from his. If his other hand wasn't holding my hip, I feel like it would have pushed me backward into the mirror. "If you died, I'd never hear you moan again."

He slams into me again, making me reach out and grip the side of his stomach. Then he begins fucking me slowly, but hard and deep. We moan together, enjoying the slow pace he sets. His deep thrusts are making my legs shake with pleasure, but I don't want to come this quickly.

"Fuck." He grunts, fingers digging into my hips. "I almost lost you." His hand abandons the task of holding my head and moves to join his other hand on my hips. He has forgotten the pace and his thrusts becomes fast and erratic.

My brows furrow as my head drops back, crying out. His fingers move between us, and his index finger finds my clit, rubbing it. It sets me off into a moaning fit as I dig my nails into his shoulders. "Stop! It's too sensitive!"

He doesn't listen. The intense pressure rakes through my legs, causing my toes to tingle. "I almost *fucking* lost you, Esmeray."

Wave of heat rushes from my head to my clit. "Daddy, please!"

"Fucking come. Come right on Daddy's cock."

I throw my head back, my hips and legs shaking. "Don't stop!" I grip the counter, and all my limbs tingle with the familiar pleasure. His fingers don't stop with the swirl of my clit as his dick thrusts harder and faster inside of me.

I fell over the edge, crying out. My body stiffens and he never stops, letting me come undone around him. Stars dance behind my eyelids as the orgasm crashes into me.

"Fuck. I'm coming." He grunts.

My eyes snap open and I look at him still in a daze. "Come for me, daddy."

He pulls out of me, fisting his cock. His dick moves at the pace that he was fucking me.

"Fuck, Daddy, please. Give it to me," I beg pathetically.

His abs flex as he lets out a low groan. Hot cum flies against my stomach and I watch in satisfaction until his moans die down and his hips cease its movements.

Rejected Wolf

Afterwards, we take our time showering and rubbing each other down. I don't know whether the orgasm he gave me was magical, but it got rid of my headache. I don't tell him that in fear of his ego getting big.

A text makes me end my shower early. Not that we aren't done. We spent most of it cleaning each other and making out a few times. I can't get enough of him.

I open the phone to see Zeno texting me.

Zeno: Hey, Mami. I'm missing you.

I smile before snapping a selfie of my back to the mirror as my arms cover my nipples and send it with a winking emoji.

He opens it instantly and answers.

Zeno*:* Fuck. Now I really miss you.

I bit my lip. Surely, he knows that I just had sex with Stone, but he doesn't seem to care.

Me: If only you came for pizza.

Zeno*:* If I would have known it was that kind of pizza, I would have come over. I could have joined you guys.

Stone gets out, grabbing a towel. I show Stone the picture. "Sent this to Zeno," I say.

He licks his lips. "It's hot, baby." It's still weird to see how okay he is with sharing me with his friends.

I think back to what Zeno had texted. *I could have joined.* "Would you have fucked me in front of Zeno?"

He raises a brow. "Yes, why?"

"Just still mind blowing," I mutter. It is. I was all over Krew this morning and not one of them seemed to have a problem. I'm still not used to Stone being okay with sharing.

I text Zeno back, thinking about each one of our kisses.

Me: You don't understand how badly I want you, Z.

Zeno: Z?

I smirk.

Me: Sorry, Papi. I want you.

Zeno: Soon, baby. I promise you won't be disappointed.

I bite my lip. I take a few more pictures and send it to him, all very sexy, but not enough to reveal everything.

Me: Think about me when you masturbate tonight, Papi.

Zeno: Way ahead of you.

Zeno texts back before sending a picture of his sweating abs and his hand right over his tip, so I can't see it. Stone shakes his head, chuckling and leaving the bathroom.

Me: Tease!

65

Rejected Wolf

Zeno: Please, Mami. All those pictures are teasing.

Before I can reply, he sends a voice message. I bite my lip, lowering my volume and pulling the phone to my ear.

"Oh, Mami. You don't realize how much I want you." It starts with Zeno's deep voice and his panting. Heat pools in my stomach as I rub my thighs together. I can hear his wet fist moving faster as he moans my name over and over. "I'm coming, Mami. I'm coming, Mami."

I fan myself, panting and feeling myself getting wet again.

He lets out a final moan, saying "Esmeray," as he comes. Its takes me a second to recover from that before I text him back.

Me: Fuckkkkk. How dare you tease me like that?

Zeno: Did you like?

Me: Yessss!

Zeno: Now I need to shower.

I bit my lip.

Me: Send me pictures!

Zeno: Will do, Mami.

I take a few more pictures before leaving the bathroom and going into the bedroom.

"You guys need to fuck already. The sexual tension is too much." I snort when Stone says that. I sit on the bed, drying my body before we finally watch movies and relax for the rest of the night.

I wake up the next day to Stone's alarm going off at eight a.m. *Fucker. How dare he wake me up?*

He rolls over, turning it off. "I'm going for a run."

I groan. "Fuck off." Although I am glad, he feels good enough to go running like we used to.

He chuckles, leaning over and kissing my lips lightly. "I'll be back for your ass in a few hours."

I watch him leave before turning over. Then my phone goes off for a video call. Begrudgingly, I answer it. "What?"

Krew's eyes light up the screen. "Are you awake?"

I grumble, "No." I blink a few times before noticing his eyes are wet, red, and puffy. I sit up really quickly. "What's wrong?"

"Sorry. I woke you. Can I come over? I want to talk."

I bite my lip. "Mhm. Are you driving? Can you even drive?"

"Kai will be taking me. Apparently, he wants to work out with Stone." Krew chuckles. "He needs it."

I don't laugh like he probably wants me to. Nerves rises in my guts. "Okay, text me when you are close. I'm gonna put on clothes."

"You don't have to." He's silent for a moment, before I cackle.

Rejected Wolf

"Okay. Hurry up. I'll be naked."

His eyes light up as he says, "On my way now." He hangs up.

I chew on my lip. *What could he possibly want to talk about?* I get up and dress into short shorts and a crop top before trying to fix my face and hair. I brush my teeth and even put on deodorant.

Before I even enter the bedroom, there's a knock. I rush to the door, throwing it open.

Krew's eyes run down my body. "Disappointed."

Rolling my eyes, I pull him inside and close the door behind him. "Shut up. What's wrong?"

He let out a sigh, sitting on the bed before shooting up. "Did you guys fuck here?"

"No... It was in the bathroom."

His eyes drift to the bathroom, smirking. "Oh." *Should I have not said that?* He sits but doesn't start talking. Instead, he takes the last piece of pizza from the nightstand and takes a bite out of it. "Mhm."

"Krew," I snap.

His hazel eyes move up to me as he swallows. "I... I said some horrible things to you. I just want to know if you forgave me already and why you would."

He was crying over our fight. I move to the bed and sit beside him. "Because no matter how big the fight is, I will always forgive you."

He shakes his head. "Do you actually forgive me or was it because of me dying?"

Truly his words and actions still hurt, but I don't care. Maybe it is because he basically almost died that made me care about him more. "I-I don't know. Does it matter?"

"So, if I wasn't dying, would you forgive me?" He stands so quickly I get dizzy.

"I forgave you instantly. I just wanted you to forgive yourself," I snap.

Krew stares at me before sighing. "Stupid fuck is in my head again."

I blink. "Who? Reed?"

He nods. "He came by this morning…"

I stand, moving to him. Grabbing his cheeks, I guide him so he's looking at me. "Please don't listen to him. I forgave you the moment I left your room at the academy. It hurt to have you ignore me, but I gave you space."

"I've… You don't understand. I've never felt this before." He lets out a sigh.

My brows pull together. "Huh?"

He leans down, taking my lips softly. I keep my hands on his cheeks. "I have a pull to you."

I bite away a laugh. "Oh, really?"

He rolls his eyes. "I said some really hurtful things to you because I listened to Reed saying you'd never be with me. I lied to Stone about liking you. I didn't even know this was a pull until you were with the pack at the hospital, and it felt like I could get better. Having you touch me, kiss my cheek. It… gave me hope. I wanted to fight to get back to you, so I can tell you, I want you and that I'm sorry about… the night of the party."

My eyes scan his face. Being reminded of that night makes my chest hurt. I caught him about to fuck someone else. "Do you want me like you wanted her or—"

He cuts me off. "I was trying to fuck her to get my mind off you. I didn't even want her. I wanted you. I don't care about sharing you, as long as I get the piece of you that was meant for me. I would rather go the rest of my life with you and a million mates than without you."

My heart swells. "Fuck."

He smirks with a chuckle, "Fuck…"

"This is why you were crying?"

"Because I didn't want to live without you."

My eyes tear up. "Don't be stupid."

He cups my face, bringing my eyes back up to his beautiful face. Krew's the opposite of what you want. He's the pretty fuck boy that makes your knees weak when he smiles. His hair is short and dirty blonde on the top that is slightly longer and curlier. His chin is sharp, leading down the massive number of muscles he has. He's like Stone, but less wide and slightly tan, especially now that he's feeling better. He breaks hearts. He broke mine. But when he kisses me again, I forget about it. "I'd do anything to call you mine. Please..."

I nod. "One rule, we don't have sex until I know you're serious about us. I don't want to be another fuck."

He nods. "You'd never be anyways."

Stone

I feel Esmeray's nerves rising in my chest through our
bond. It has developed between us more and more with
each time we sleep together. Even talking to her makes
it grow, though not as strong. I take a deep breath to
settle my own before looking over at her.

Esmeray looks up at me, chewing on her
bottom lip before taking a deep breath to calm herself.
She's getting good at that, but I have to give her a look
to make sure she knows we can feel it. It's best for the
alpha to not feel like that. They are our leading
example.

Rune Hunt

I found her this morning with Krew, but she was sleeping on his chest. Surprising, they weren't naked, and it didn't smell like sex. They were just sleeping and cuddling.

I'm even more surprised Krew was doing that. He's never been into cuddling with anyone. He's the type to fuck someone and move on very quickly. But Kai told me what Reed did this morning about Esmeray. Krew seems to be feeling bad about what he did to her.

She forgave him. I'm not sure if I could be quick to do that, but between this formal interview and the shifting issue, she has too much on her plate to not forgive him.

We walk into the city hall in the town nearby. From the outside, you'd never know it was run by wolves. I open the door for her and the others.

Esmeray smiles up at me, and I keep a smile on my lips until I get to Reed. If I was Alpha, I would have ditched him a long time ago. But Esmeray has a pull with him and that's the only thing keeping him around, or I would have beaten his ass over the shit he's pulling.

Kai leads her towards the council room which is front and center in the building. I see my father with my family outside the room. He's dressed in a fancy suit like my own. We are dressed all nicely. The air sweetened when she saw us. She liked it, more than she admitted.

Rejected Wolf

My dad smiles at us. Esmeray has taken a liking to him, I suspect it's because she lost hers and was close to him before. She likes my mother, but Esmeray's left her soon after her birth, so she can't relate as much with her. My father hugs me when we approach.

"Hey," I mutter. He pats my back. He's been to council meetings a million times, and he always said his first was nerve-racking.

He pulls back, hugging the others. "How are you guys? Nervous?"

Esmeray shakes her head, and I know she's not lying. Either she's good at hiding her feelings or she's really okay. "I think we are okay, no matter what the fuck they want to talk about," she says.

Zeno touches her back. Her lack of nerves now can be that she has four mates backing her up.

I glance at my father. He seems to notice, but it doesn't bother him. He was the first to suspect that she might have more than one mate. I didn't care either way. She was still mine too, no matter what she does with the others.

Smelling her after Zeno turned her on last night is something I'd like to experience again. I don't mind watching or joining. When we were with Kai, I watched. She was different than she was with me. With me, she pushed me to do a lot more. Kai may or may not be into that.

Rune Hunt

The door opens for us, and someone steps out to tell us the council is ready for us. This time, I grab Esme's hand and let her take the reins. I would follow her blindly to the ends of the earth.

Esmeray

I've been to court before and this is what court exactly feels like. A bunch of men—one in the middle—looking at you and judging you. My pack sits at a table in the middle of the room while Silver and his family sit behind in the rows of seats. The only thing missing is the jury and is the girl who types what we say on the weird computer thing.

"Esmeray," Michael greets.

I bow my head a bit. He wasn't in the middle, so I looked at the one in the middle. "I don't think we've met."

"My name is Ricardo Morales. My men beside me are Robert, Michael, Brick, James, Jack and Isaac."

"Are you all alphas?"

Ricardo nods his head, his short curls falling against his forehead. "We are the founding Alphas of Arizona. Do you know why you all are here today?"

Rejected Wolf

I push hair behind my ear. "You probably suspect we have some involvement with the attack on Moon Born Academy."

He nods. "We will get to that. First, have you shifted before?"

I feel like a complete liar when I shake my head. *But why would I ever feel like a liar?* I would have known if I ever shifted. Kai said he remembers each time when I asked before. "No, sir. I wasn't at Moon Born long enough to learn how."

He clears his throat. "I know your circumstance were different, as you didn't have your parents to guide you into your first shift. Sometimes, it's easier to have friends shift with you so it's more... enjoyable. There's obvious evidence of you being a shifter and an alpha. Do you know what I'm talking about?"

"The mark? The threads? The bonds?"

He nods, standing and rounding the counter to a television off to the side. "But there's other evidence as well. Would you like to see?"

I nod.

He presses a button on the stand before leaning against a table and letting us watch it.

I lean forward, watching what looks like the mess hall. I noticed the huge mountain of man standing with his back to the camera. His hands are embedded into Kira's dreads and watching him do that again pisses me off. It was from the day I left early with Kira after my phone was broken.

In the video, I snap at him, reeling a loud harsh growl from my throat. *I can do that…*

Stone stiffens beside me while Krew shudders.

In the video, I grab his wrist and begin speaking low to him before I finally bang my hand against the table, and he jumps. The guy who is at least two feet taller than me *jumps.* I say something to him again, rolling my shoulder before he looks down. I turn looking at someone. My eyes are pure white before I blink, looking around with my normally dark eyes again before leaving with Kira.

Goosebumps raise on my arms as Ricardo rewinds it to where my eyes were a pure smoky white. I hear the council member mutter before it silences.

"Explain," Ricardo says.

"I—I… I don't think—I don't even remember interacting with him. I remember talking to Kira and leaving with Kira."

"Why is that?"

I shrug, nerves begin to set in with confusion. *What did I do? Why were my eyes that color? Kira said I didn't hurt him…* "He broke my phone. I remember that and when I get upset sometimes… I black out…"

"So, you've blacked out before?" Michael asks as Ricardo begins to sit down.

"A few times. It's rare."

"Why is this important?" Stone asks.

I'm wondering the same shit.

"Motives, really," Michael says as he moves to the table in front of us with files in his hands. "So, when you were fourteen, do you remember harming a woman to within an inch of her life?"

It's so silent that you can hear a pin drop.

I feel eyes burning into me as my blood runs cold. *They… went through my record? Of course, they did. They think I'm a threat. It doesn't make sense for me to be a threat, though.* I stare at him silently as I start picking at my nails below the table.

He opens the file, setting it down with a picture of a girl in a hospital on top of the stack. The girl was twenty-one at the time. The picture makes her face look unrecognizable. Her jaw is wired shut and swollen to the size of the balloon. Her eyes are blackened and sunken in while her swollen cheek has a claw mark on it.

Instead of cracking under pressure like all cops tried to get me to do, numbness runs over me. It's the feeling you get when you are outside in the snow for too long and pins and needles have taken over your limbs. But for me, it's all over my body. "I remember the aftermath, not the action they accused me of doing. Next question?"

"Do you know your family has a history of violence?"

I scoff. "I don't know if my mother and my father was the nicest people ever. Do you think I came to Moon Born for a planned attack? Why would I do that?"

He shrugs. "There's a rumor that you might have known you were a shifter and planned with Midnight wolves for the fall of Moon Born."

I roll my eyes. "I didn't even know this place existed."

Michael raises a brow, glancing at Ricardo. "How did you have influence on Mr. Thorne?"

I let out a heated breath, sitting on my fingertips to get feeling back. "Who?"

"Mr. Brock Thorne?" he repeats.

I blink again.

"Mountain man," Stone whispers to me.

Oh... Him. "I don't know. Was it really an influence or was he scared of me?"

Michael shakes his head. "He listened to you to the point where he turned himself into the dean and asked to be removed because he didn't feel safe."

I shrug. "That made two of us. Three, if you count Kira. Now, please, get to the point. I'm very confused on where this is going."

"The Midnight Academy seems to think you are the reincarnated version of Luna. A Goddess Alpha, if you will. If they believe that they might see you as a threat or a really good accomplice."

I raise a brow, stifling a laugh.

"Esmeray, Moon born Academy has never been attacked before in the hundreds of years it's been

Rejected Wolf

running. Now almost ten students are dead, but you and Krew are alive. Why is that?"

I shrug. "You guys tell me. Seems like you know everything." I should bite my tongue, but I can't.

"Esmeray," Ricardo says, drawing my attention to him. "We don't mean to make you upset. We just want to make sure you guys have nothing to do with it."

I roll my eyes. "I assure you a hundred percent my pack had nothing to do with that attack. I know the attackers mentioned some crazy things, but we knew nothing about what was going to happen."

He eyes me hard, and I eye him right back.

"So, you don't think you're the Goddess reincarnated?"

I snort. "I'm just Esmeray Devine. The alpha that hasn't shifted. I'm more focused on that."

Ricardo nods, "I think it's safe to say that you should be able to shift with the help of your pack by the time Moon Born opens after Halloween."

"Or you and your pack won't be allowed back at Moon Born again," Michael says.

Mutters run through the room as my chest is tightening. I have about three months to shift. I couldn't even shift in the eighteen years of my life. Three months?

"Come on!" Krew huffs. I lean back, sending him a look that says, "It's okay." His jaw tightens. He

80

doesn't seem to be phased that I beat a twenty-one-year-old at fourteen. Thank god. I'm worried about what Kai or Zeno will think of me now? Reed is going to have a field day with this.

"Agreed?" Ricardo asks.

I just nod, chewing on my lip.

"I'll be watching, Esmeray."

"That was brutal…" Krew huffs, making Kai mutter with agreement as we leave the room.

My shoulder burns like someone lit a fire on it. I reach up as Zeno and Krew hold open the doors to the waiting room for me and for the next person going in.

The air stiffens and all I can smell are my mates. Stone with his cedar wood, Kai with his orange, Krew with his ocean spray, Zeno with his mint, and even Reed with his expensive ass cologne. But there's another. It reminds me of the smell of freshly cut grass.

A smothering gaze burns into me, making me look up.

The fire belongs to the gaze of a guy, and I get lost in his dark lust filled eyes. I want to pry my eyes way, but I can't. Something about this moment feels mesmerizing. He's wearing what looks like a black prison jumpsuit of some sort. Tattoos crawl from each part of the hems. One is against his Adam's apple as he lifts his head a bit. Stubble of dark hair has grown on his chin and above his full lips. There's a small scar over his nose and blacken eyelid. His dark hair is short, curling a bit against his forehead.

Iron cuffs sit around his wrists, which have more tattoos on them leading to his fingers. The cuffs are chained to a collar on his neck that is also connected to an iron muzzle around his jaw, lips and nose.

But I can see the soft curl of a smile, curling further as he looks at me.

Slowly, we pass each other, his arm brushing mine and igniting a fire within me. And when goosebumps raise against my skin, I twist around to see him. He does the same, letting his eyes wander down my body, taking me in before he gives me a boyish smirk that makes me snap forward.

I hear the doors close behind me, clearing the air of *whatever* that was. I rub the burning sensation from my shoulder.

"What was that?" Zeno asks me, lowly near my ear.

I shrug.

"Did you know him?"

Now that he mentioned it, that guy did look familiar, but I'm not sure how. "Maybe…" But the more I think about him, the more my stomach swirls. They can smell me… My mates will know a random stranger just turned me on.

Once we get outside, Silver hugs Stone and says we can talk more about it at the house.

I nod.

Meeting at the house... Great.

Something stands out to me while remembering that video from the cafeteria. It weighs heavily on my chest because I feel like I know the answer. "Reed," I say, not even looking at him. "Did you record that video?"

All of my mates stop, looking at me.

"Did you almost kill that girl like they said?" he retorts.

"Yes," I say honestly. "Now you answer."

"Why did you do it?"

Anger raises within me. "Why did *you* do it?!" I twist around, looking up at the fucker. He recorded that video and I know he did.

He smiles down at me. "You know, Esmeray. You've been so insecure lately. Are you that suspicious that I would do that to you?"

I roll my eyes. "You think that is low? After *fucking* calling me names and putting me down? You think recording me would be *fucking* low?"

"Why would I give it to them?" Reed snaps. "I hate them as much as anyone else does."

I take a deep breath. "I swear to god, if you had anything to do with this, I'll—"

"You'll what? Get on your knees and take my dick into your mouth? Bend over to fuck you like Stone—"

Rejected Wolf

"Shut up!" Krew snaps as growling comes from his throat and his pupils thin like they do when they shift.

"You've said enough, Reed," Zeno mutters.

"She's playing you guys and you guys couldn't be more blind! She almost killed someone."

I roll my eyes. "I was going to explain it when we got back to Stone's, asshole. She threatened my life."

He snorts. "Sure, and what about that guy?"

The guy... My face softens but anger raises inside of me. "That mountain?!"

"The guy your 'dad' killed!" he snaps.

"Enough!" I snap, glaring at him through frosty eyes. "My father would never hurt someone. You didn't know him like I did!"

He cocks a brow.

"What are you even talking about, Reed?" Kai asks.

But his dark eyes are locked onto me. "We both know who actually did it, Esmeray."

I roll my eyes, walking to the truck. "Fuck off, Reed. I have no idea what you're talking about."

Reed snorts. "She's hiding so much from you love struck idiots. I, for one, am not going to get played." He leaves, just like he did in my dream.

I blink away the gloss over my eyes, feeling a pounding headache start on again. Everything feels so

84

overwhelming that it's making my chest tighten. "Let's go."

Esmeray

"We need a game plan," Silver starts when we're seated around the table.

"First," I interject. "I need to say something." My pack sits around the table minus Reed, but plus Kira. She came as support and help for me. I appreciated it dearly. "I was fourteen when I beat up that twenty-one-year-old."

"Twenty-one?" Krew snorts.

"She came at me with a knife. I think she was cracked out on some type of drug or whatever. At first, I was charged with battery, but they soon dropped that when video evidence showed that she attacked me first." I watch all their faces, waiting for them to react like Reed, yet no one did. "It's just something I don't like to talk about it because when I blackout, I don't know what I do to people."

Kai nods. "I think it's called a white out at this point, if it's anything like what happened when you yelled at Reed."

My brows pull together.

Zeno leans against the wall near me. "Your eyes went completely white when you got pissed."

I chew on my bottom lip. "Did the same with the mountain man…" Nerves fill me. This feels like a huge overwhelming mess.

Zeno touches my back assuring me he's there for me.

"They will do anything to hold it against you," Silver says, touching his chin.

"Why am I a threat?"

He shrugs. "You are different and attracting unwanted attention. They could actually think you're working with Midnight and demon wolves. I don't think you're an actual threat. For the most part, you seem to stay out of trouble."

I nod. "Try to."

"Plan, Alpha?" Kai asks.

I look at Silver who looks at me. "Oh. Yeah. Uh… So, I have to shift before Halloween at the latest. So, we train, and we try every day. I want to learn how to fight in my human form, so if an attack ever happens again, I'm prepared. I'm assuming if I haven't shifted by now, it has to be forced out."

Silver nods. "Krew and Stone are the best at hand-to-hand combat while Zeno is better with weapons. Kai is better at the mental aspect, so he will help you learn about your wolf and call it out. You're missing a lot of the senses that wolves have. Super scent, hearing, and even feeling."

"I can help with that too," Zeno says behind me.

"I doubt Reed will help us…"

"Give Reed time," Silver says with a sigh.

It's getting to the point that I'm tired of waiting for him. Everyone makes excuses for him and says for him to have more time. Soon I'm going to tell him to get his ass into gear or stay out of my way. "Can we start tomorrow? I am exhausted and would love to just relax."

Silver gives me a shrug. "Esmeray, you are the alpha; you decide what's best."

I look down at my hands. Part of me knows that I should start working today to get ahead of our enemies but with everything that happened today, I just don't want to try, fail, and become frustrated.

Zeno leans into me, letting his heat covering my back. He puts his lips near my ear and whispers, "It's okay to take tonight to think." His voice sounds like velvet in my ear. That sends heat into my stomach.

I clear my throat. "Yeah. I think we should have a night to just breathe for a second before things get... real."

Silver nods, basically dismissing us.

Doubt runs through me as I turn and go around Zeno to leave. *If I were Silver, would I have chosen to start today with the training?* My life is in danger with these demon wolves and the Midnight wolves. Now, the council thinks I'm bringing trouble to the little perfect world they have.

I'm not sure how I should go about this right now. All I know is, I have to shift by October, and I don't even know where to begin. I feel more lost than I ever have been. So many questions buzz around my head and not enough answers.

Too much stress in being Alpha.

Stone grabs my hand just before I get to my room. I didn't even notice all of them following me to my room. And it's not even for the reason that I want... no fivesome in my future. "Hey, let's talk about this. You don't have to have all the stress on yourself."

I reach up, rubbing the back of my neck. "Kind of do. I'm Alpha."

Kai shakes his head. "But that doesn't mean what you want it to be. These last few weeks have been a weird adjustment period. Stuff seems like... they are starting to bother you."

I blink at him

89

Rejected Wolf

Of course, things are bothering me. I met you guys, not even knowing this would happen. Reed is a dick. Krew had someone else's mouth on his dick. The dream about Reed rejecting me is coming true and the voice telling me to figure out who I am and remember when I shifted and it doesn't make any sense. "I can do this, guys."

Stone raises a brow. "Esmeray, you don't have to do this alone. We are a team."

I bit my lip only to hold back a laugh. "Well... want to take a bath as a team? Because I plan on taking the longest fucking bath in my life."

Krew's hazel eyes light up, lust running down my body. "If you insist."

Stone hits his chest, stopping him from coming inside the room.

"She said—"

I take a deep breath. "I can do this, right?"

They all speak at once, throwing encouragement my way. It feels nice to always know that no matter how many twenty-one-years-olds I beat up, they'll have my back through it all.

Kai ducks between Stone and Krew. "I'll draw your bath." I watch him turn the corner to the bathroom. Kai is the smallest out of the group, but when it comes to muscles, definitely not in the downstairs department. What he lacks in muscles, he has in other places. He's also the smartest and the

90

kindest one of them all. Zeno is kind, but I've seen his grades. He needs help. Krew is the worst. *Poor guy.*

Stone places a kiss against my lips. "I'll let you relax tonight. Call me if you need me."

I touch his shoulders, using them as leverage to reach up to kiss him. "Good night, Stone."

He winks at me.

Zeno pushes Stone out the way to get to me. He wraps his arms around my waist, pulling me right into his heat. "Can I have one?"

I tilt my head back, looking up at him. "Take one."

He grabs the back of my head, his other hand pulling me into his chest by the waist. My eyes widen as he crushes his lips into mine. I run my hand up his chest to his jaw. Our lips move together so perfectly, it's like we've kissed more than one time. Heat pools in my stomach. He pulls back, leaving me gasping and aching for more. "Good night, Mami."

I lick my lips as he goes to Stone's room. I wonder if he plans on staying over tonight. I wonder if he knew how much I wanted him, yet is walking away from me. *Like what?*

"Do I get one?" Krew's voice snaps me from my daze.

I glance down at his body, loving his looks in nice pants and a dress down shirt. His hands are his pocket as a sheepish smile stays on his lips. "No."

He nods, smiling still. "Fair enough."

Rejected Wolf

But before he can leave, I grab his button up, pulling him flush against me. I lay my lips right on his, quickly. It's enough to spark those feelings in me that I have for him. We stay close to each other, even if we barely touch each other. Our breathing is heavy as if we just kissed for a while. But the kiss was so brief, it feels like it barely happened. His hands finally move, touching my waist softly.

"This... is going to be hard," I whisper, more to myself.

He licks his lips, dropping his eyes to my lips. "But... it'll be worth it, Esme." He pulls me close to feel his hard dick right across my stomach, close to my sternum. "Go fuck Kai, make yourself come, and forget the world for a while. I'll be thinking about you tonight."

Then he moves from me. My body misses his warmth instantly. *They had decided Kai was going to sleep with me tonight. Or was it my conscious choice?* They all look so yummy today, but I can't have them all. Krew and I are on this weird break type thing. Maybe... Kai needs me tonight.

I close and lock the door, hearing the rushing water from the bathroom. I unhook my skirt before dropping it. Stepping out of it and throwing my shirt over my head, I glance down at myself. I'm in a lacy black bra and panties with my black boot heels still on. *Damn... Kai better not reject me, or I'd end up just pleasing myself because I look hot.*

Rune Hunt

Leaning against the door frame of the bathroom. I peer inside, seeing Kai bent over to agitate the water for the bubbles. His sleeves are rolled up to his elbows, showing his veiny arms, and his pants are tight around his firm ass. His white hair falls over his eyes as he looks down at the bath. "Damn…" I mutter to myself.

He straightens, moving from the water. "I put bubbles in the water for—" His hazel eyes finally land on me, swiping over my curves and my breasts. He definitely is a boob kind of guy. Stone is an ass guy. Zeno seems to not mind either while Krew might be into feet. "Fuck."

I tilt my head like I'm innocent. "What?"

He smiles with a chuckle, unable to form words.

I move to him, touching his forearms. "See something you like?"

He licks his lips. "Mhm."

"Want to join me in the bath?"

He slightly shakes his head. "You should be relaxing, baby girl. Not... doing this."

I kick off my heels, pushing my bottom lip out. "You don't want me?"

"Esmeray," he warns.

I reach around, unhooking my bra and dropping it slowly. His eyes instantly move to my breasts, eating them up. His hand clenches and I can tell he's holding back, but why? *Does he really think I'm this fragile?* I hook a finger in my underwear and drop them.

Still, he doesn't touch me.

"Are you going to make me please myself?"

He licks his lips again.

I shrug, stepping into the perfectly warm water and sink into the bubbles. I lift one of my legs over the side of the tub, index fingers finding my clit. I hiss, dropping my head back to the tub lightly. I swirl my fingers until my toes feel that familiar tingling feeling. "Please, Kai. Come join me." My eyes drop to his crotch. With a free hand, I reach out to touch the hardness in his pants.

"Fuck," he drags out, working on his shirt while I get to my knees to help him with his pants. He's barely halfway done before I get his cock free and run my tongue against the salty tip. He lets out a breath of air as I suck on his tip, running my tongue over his hole. I taste his precum and I want to taste his cum in the worst way.

He rips his clothes off, completely naked in front of me. I run my hand up his flat stomach, shoving his cock into my throat, deeply. But I move back, looking up at him. "Come fuck me, Kai."

He smirks, fisting his cock, drawing my eyes to it. "Maybe I should tease you like you do me."

"Please do," I mutter, watching his hand run up and down himself.

I moan out.

But he stops, holding out his hand. "Spit, baby."

I accumulate spit in my mouth before slowly spitting into his hand. He runs it over his cock, rubbing it in. With that, he begins to pump. "Fuck," I mutter, glancing up to see him watching me. I move back, running hands over my bubbly breasts. "Kai."

He bites his lip. "Fuck it, I need you. Kneel on the side."

I listen, kneeling on the small seat in the tub and letting my body hang over the side. He steps in the tub, grabbing my ass and pulling me up a bit. Before I can even say anything, he slams into my wet pussy. I grip the edge, hissing.

He rubs my ass, trying to distract me from the pain. "You do look so good from the back. Stone was right."

I twist around. "What?"

He smiles at me with a boyish grin like his brother has sometimes. "We were talking about your ass today. No big deal."

My jaw drops. "Kai! You?"

He shrugs, lifting his hand and letting it drop against my ass with a crack. "Are you ready, baby?"

I wiggle my ass, feeling his cock reach spots it didn't before. Doggie style just makes everything feel so much better.

He takes that as a *yes*, pulling out and slowly going back into me. He goes slow at first, earning moans. He doesn't rush it no matter how many times I throw myself back into him. Still, he lets me adjust until I'm whimpering and begging for more.

"More?" He runs a hand up my spine to my hair and fists it.

Kai has never been rough with me. He's been the complete opposite from what the others are. He's soft and gentle, scared to hurt me. But apparently his talk with Stone made him so much more comfortable.

"Please," I beg, and when he lets go of my hair, my head drops. His hands grip my waist, and he begins fucking me hard and fast. With each thrust, my breasts bounce and water splashes against the side of the tub, some trickling over. I grip the edge, moaning out. "Fuck, yes!"

I push myself against him, before reaching back and grabbing his hip. He takes advantage of that and grabs my wrist, putting it against the small of my back and pushing me into the side of the tub more.

He uses my wrist to pull me back into him, slamming hard into me.

"Fuck!" I cry out as a familiar tightness builds up in my hips. "I'm so close, Kai!"

His thrust became irate, and I can tell by the swelling and twitching of his cock that he's close too.

Lust has completely clouded my mind, glazing over my eyes. "Please don't stop. Please don't stop."

"I won't, baby. I won't."

"I'm coming!" I cry.

Rune Hunt

He listens, thrusting until finally I shatter around him, coming undone. My cries bounce off the walls as a huge wave of heat washes over me. Stars dance behind my eyes as I dig my nails into his stomach.

He grinds himself into me, groaning into my ear until he finally stiffens and shudders. I feel his hot semen fill me, spilling down my leg. "Fuck," he drags out, satisfaction filling his voice.

He helps me sit where I was kneeling as he sits at the bottom of the tub where my feet are. "Are you okay? Was I too rough?"

I chuckle. "That was amazing. I like it when you take charge."

He smiles, looking down. He runs a hand over his sweaty hair, pushing it back from his forehead. The smile soon fades.

I move from the ledge, wrapping my legs around his waist and sitting on his lap. "Are you okay?"

"I think I have to buy you the morning after pill now..." he mutters, clearly lost in his thoughts.

I completely forgot about it for a second. I want to enjoy his semen inside of me... It filled me with warmth when he came. I almost let out a laugh. I might have a breeding kink apparently. "Can you sit with me for a while? I'd like to relax with you."

He looks up, eyes locking with mine. Although Krew and Kai are twins and have hazel eyes, Kai's are a little bluer than Krew's. He stretches, kissing my lips. I wrap my arms around his shoulders. Might as well take advantage of him being able to come inside of me a few times more.

Esmeray

Honk!

A loud horn springs me from the bed, scrambling to grab blankets to cover my naked body which in turn pulls them from Kai.

I glance over with wide eyes at Krew who glances down at his brother's naked body. "Dear god!" Krew covers his eyes. "Thank god, we aren't exactly twins!"

They are... I grab the pillow and whip it at Krew. "What the fuck?" I put blankets back over Kai, who is just now waking up.

Rejected Wolf

"Time to train, beautiful," Krew says, uncovering his eyes. His eyes land straight on the Plan B package on the nightstand. He grabs the empty box, throwing it at Kai. "Told you, you didn't know how to pull out."

Kai winces, throwing it back. "Fuck off, dick!"

I roll my eyes, flopping back on the bed.

"Esmeray! Up now!" Krew barks at me, making me fucking laugh. *Who does he think he is?* The bed shifts under his weight as he jumps on me lightly.

I giggle, trying to push him off, but he straddles my hips.

Then he bounces up and down on my stomach and hips. "Up! Up!"

I push him. "You are a kid!" But he doesn't budge so I pull him down, locking my legs around his waist. "Stop! Stop! I'm up!"

He freezes, painfully aware now that I am fully naked, like he didn't know before. His eyes drop to the top of my breasts, almost spilling out from the blankets. He adjusts, lowering his hips from my core and pushing the blankets to my collarbones. "Time to become the alpha wolf you can be, Esme."

My eyes search his face. "You think I'm going to do good today?"

He chuckles, his warm breath hitting my neck from how low he is. "No. Not today."

My smile fades, and I roll my eyes.

100

"But every day, you'll get stronger, and you'll become better than you were the day before."

My breath hitches. He's being so kind and genuine.

His eyes shift from mine to my lips, but before I can even try to kiss him, he reaches behind his back, unlocking my legs and standing. "Five minutes to get downstairs. Get up!" He grabs the air horn, honking it at a sleeping Kai once more before leaving.

Kai barely flinches, probably used to this shit.

I got ready in six minutes, earning a scowl from Krew that I ignored.

Zeno hands me over a water bottle and a packet of pre-workout. I huff. "So, we are serious about this?"

"Yes," Stone says behind me, voice booming as he jogs down the steps. "Take it. You'll need it."

Instead of mixing the packet into the water like a normal human, I empty it into my mouth, eyes locked on Stone. He smirks as I swish it around my mouth with water before swallowing.

"Good fucking girl." Stone slaps my ass. "Now, move to the gym."

I barely flinch at the spank. "Huh? Gym?"

So, Silver has a fucking huge ass gym in the house. It has almost all of the equipment and then times that by two, because there's double than a normal gym.

Rejected Wolf

"So, game plan," Stone says, shedding out of his shirt. His muscles flex and relax with each movement. I don't hide my wandering eyes. He's obviously used the gym quite a few times. "Focus, Esmeray."

Slowly, I pry my eyes back to his. "I can't work like this. You have your elbows out, whore."

Krew chuckles beside me as Stone tries not to.

"Esmeray…" Zeno warns.

I raise a brow. "Watch the tone, Z, before I go to HR and tell them what you've been doing. I just simply can't work like this, sorry."

"What's HR?" Krew questions silently.

Kai chuckles. "Don't make him think too early, baby, or he'll be fried by the end of the day."

I smirk, earning a look from Krew.

"Esmeray," Zeno warns again, drawing my attention.

"Okay. Okay. Game plan, boss."

Stone cross his arms over his muscular chest, showing off his traditional moon and wolf chest piece. I never asked him about it yet, but I'd like to know what all his tattoos mean—what all theirs mean. "Stretch, cardio, then lift. Breakfast, then brain shit with Kai, break for lunch before you train with Zeno, Krew and me. After dinner, you're free. It's not gonna be like this every day, but that's how it'll go today."

I nod. "I haven't worked out in… honestly, I've never really worked out before besides like high school where you have to."

Stretching is something I can do better than they do. I'm more flexible than the lunks of muscles are. I have never worked out much. Working in a diner, drinking a gallon of water, and running around kept me in shape.

Zeno does cardio with me on the bike. You know... I never realized how fucking hard it is to ride a bike. I rarely did it, besides my motorcycle and I never had to peddle that. I am able to keep up with Stone but with minimal breaks. By minimal, I mean a minimum of ten breaks in thirty minutes.

After cardio, Stone lets me have a break. Sweat clings to my body, making me sticky.

I'm the alpha, I could say that this is over in a heartbeat and go order pizza with Stone's card. But he'd hate me more than he does right now. Flirting with him makes everything better even if he sends me looks, but he never stops me.

We focus on upper arms. My weights were definitely lighter than Stones by, like, seventy-pounds lighter. If he didn't have such a big dick, I would have thought he was on steroids. During my small bench presses, he encourages me, corrects my form by running his hand over my thighs and biceps. When I am done, he claps for me, making me smile.

Rejected Wolf

It's not until he benches that I feel less superior to him. He can bench me, that's for sure. Zeno was his spotter, knowing if drops that amount of weight on him, I'd have to let him die. There's no way I can help.

We all exercise together for the next hour, encouraging each other and spotting each other. It almost feels like all my stress is gone for the moment. When we leave the gym room, I'm drenched in sweat and smelling gross, but I feel good. Lighter. I definitely took my anger out in there.

Anger at the council, Reed and Moon Born.

Stone leads us to the kitchen for breakfast that his mother is already making. "Protein shake?" he questions, and I nod. They drink that all the time but I'm not sure if I'll like it.

I nod a *good morning* to Liza who is almost done cooking breakfast with Ivory, Stone's youngest sister.

Ding!

My phone goes out and part of me wishes it is Reed. *Why would I wish for him to text me? Maybe to say sorry to me.*

Kira: Good morning. How's the training going?

I smile.

Me: I feel half dead and it's only nine a.m. Hey, I was thinking about getting on birth control soon.

Kira: God I hate birth control. Is there a reason for this?

Before she can even let me answer, she ends,

Kira: Oh... ew... Good on you for wanting to be safe, but... ew.

I smirk, rolling my eyes. Stone gets done with the fruit and protein shake and hands me a glass. I thank him.

Kira: I'll go with you if you want.

Me: Read my mind. Just don't need a kid with all this bullshit going on.

Kira: I understand. Are you going to tell them?

Me: I've only had sex with Stone and Kai, so maybe only them right now.

Kira: How's the Reed situation?

I flip from her text message chat bubble to Reed's. It's bare because we've rarely talked to each other. My chest tightens at that.

Me: Still hates me. I still hate him.

Kira: He's a bitch. A jealous bitch.

I smirk, moving to the dining room table and sit down.

Kira: Guess who *is* texting me.

Me: *Who?*

Kira: The sweet hot French girl from our Law class. Valentin.

Me: Oh! And?

Kira: We might set up a date.

I bit my lip, barely listening to the guys around me.

Me: Don't you have to be mates to date?

Kira: Since when has those lank heads actually taken you on a date?

It makes me chuckle. Krew leans into me, watching our conversation, luckily, he doesn't see the part of us talking about the birth control. I have nothing to hide, though.

Me: Good point. Where are you guys gonna go?

Kira: To a cafe for lunch, apparently.

Me: Send me cute pictures and let me know how it goes.

Krew's arm goes around my chair, even though he went back to the conversation with the guys. He sweat smells, but definitely not as bad as me. Come to think of it, none of their sweat smell bothers me. Maybe because Stone's and Kai's smell like this when we have sex. *Is this what Krew would smell like? Would he be this... sweet?* I close my thighs. *Not the time to think about this, Esme.*

Krew glances at me with a raising brow. "Are you okay?"

"Sore. You?"

"Not sore. Luckily as a shifter, you should heal faster than most, and when you shift, you'll heal even faster."

I twist, bumping his knee with mine. "So, when should I not be sore?"

He thinks for a moment, pushing some of his curls back. I watch his thinking face, seeing his lips move to be bitten on. I want to bite on them. I glance away. *Calm it, Esme. But they all look good exercising and lifting.* I hate my hormones because the whole time, I drooled over their bulging muscles and their defined backs. "Maybe tonight, probably tomorrow." His voice brings me back to reality.

I nod. "Cool."

His eyes wander down me just as the door opens with the food's savory smell coming in. Liza is the best at cooking. I turn away, back to the front, and set down my phone.

In walks Silver from the foyer as if his wolf nose smelt his food coming. "Good morning, guys, Esme. How is the training so far?"

"Hell," I mutter, sipping the protein shake. "We've only weight trained this morning so far."

Silver nods, sitting at the head of the table. "You have to be stronger to actually punch harder."

I shrug. "Doesn't it take six pounds of pressure to knock someone out if you hit the right spot?" When it goes silent, I look up from my food that I just plated.

Silver has a shit eating grin on his face. "Why couldn't you have been my kid?"

I glance at Stone, chuckling. "Looks like your father likes me better."

107

Rejected Wolf

Stone pushes me. "Yeah, yeah"

"Who taught you that?" Kai asks, leaning against the table. His eyes scan my face waiting for my answer.

I cock a brow, confused until I realize what he's talking about and shrug. "My dad. He wanted me to be as protected as I could be. Jaws are the first and easiest place to knock someone out. Then the temple is the second, he taught me."

"I like a girl who can throw a punch," Silver says. "That's how Liza and I met."

I almost choke on my shake. "I want to hear that story."

Silver wipes his lips with a napkin. His blue eyes brighten at the story in his head. If Stone looks anything like Silver in the future, I'll be happy. "So obviously we are mates, but Liza never liked that."

She scoffs. "You were the annoying jock at Moon Born and I just wanted to focus on studies. I knew I wanted in your pack, but I hated the idea of being an alpha's mate."

My brows pull together. "Why? Wouldn't that be cool? Seems like everyone wants to be the alpha or the mate."

She shrugs. "If you have that personality of being in the spotlight. I hated the spotlight. Plus, he's a flirt! And flirted with everything that walked."

Silver nods. "Yeah... I did. The first time we kissed on the combat field, you knocked me out." He's smiling hard, eyes sparkling at the moment they had together.

"You can't go around kissing girls without consent!" Liza defends, making me smile.

"Oh please! You wanted me."

She scoffs, but it breaks into a smile afterward. They seem to be in love and here I am, falling for their son and basically nephews. They all seem so tight-knitted and strong. I glance at Stone, wondering how different things would have been if I started at Moon Born as a kid. *Would Reed have liked me more? Would Krew stop flirting with other women? Would I have been with them all? Would I have shifted already?*

I definitely don't regret meeting them, but things would have been so much easier.

I would have been a better shifter and Alpha.

Kai

"Close your eyes," I say to Esmeray. We moved to the grass area in the back yard after breakfast. Esmeray seems so interested in Silver and Liza's story, although I've heard it a million times before. It's cute—don't get me wrong—and the idea of Liza being able to put Silver in his place, makes it ten times better, but Silver gloats so much about getting the girl who never wanted him.

I got the girl who wants me and my best friends.

Esmeray sends me a weary look. "Don't let Krew push me into the pool."

I feel the others' eyes on her, but I ignore it. "I'd never, baby."

She shudders. "I like it when you call me baby…"

Oh, I know. She gets faintly turned on when I call her pet names

She inhales before closing her eyes. She leans back on her hands where we sit.

"Shifters always have heightened senses. They can hear things from a far distance, smell things that human noses can't, and feel things that humans can't."

"Can we taste things stronger? Is that why food is so good?" she asks.

"Focus," I warn. I'm glad she can't see my smile. "Let's start with hearing. What do you hear around you?"

She takes a second to think. "Uh... voices."

Stone is talking to Zeno. I can hear their conversation clearly. They are talking about the new videogame coming out and the hype surrounding it. "What are they saying?"

She throws her hands up. "I don't know. Esmeray is pretty hot, and I like fucking her. How am I supposed to know?"

"Focus," I instruct. "Relax and silence every thought in your head."

She's struggling with this; I feel doubt running down our bond.

"None of that," I whisper to her. "Just relax. You can do this. Hear the distinct voices. Notice the difference in pitch: Zeno's low voice and Stone's calmness. Only focus on that."

Her face scrunches up and she sucks her teeth. "I can't do this, Kai. It's not working."

I swallow before moving closer to her, careful not to touch her. "Okay. Let's start closer. What can you hear from me?"

She bits her bottom pink lip, and I can't help but watch her. Esmeray is so beautiful. Her jaw is the peak of her heart shaped face. Her lips are full and pink, contrasting against her evenly tan skin. There's a light tan spot around her neck, almost touching her jaw, and some around her eyes and nose. She has high cheekbones and a small button nose. Her brows are thick but perfectly sculpted. Her long lashes are together, falling against her cheeks. Her curls are up today into "space buns" as she called it. That white streak running in the middle. Her bronze, brown body has a lot of lighter skin on her, especially on her back and legs. She seems comfortable enough to wear booty shorts and a tank top though. She shrugs at my question.

"So, you don't hear my voice? My breath?" I inhale deeply to show her.

"Yeah. I hear that."

"Focus on breath, hollow in on it." I lean forward, breathing deeply right near her face.

She shudders, smirking. "I feel your breath."

"Focus on the way it enters my nose and travels into my lungs."

Her lips part, making my eyes flicker to him. I lick my lips, softly.

"I heard you lick your lips!" she says, jolting with joy. "I heard it clearer than anything because you were breathing in your mouth, not your nose."

I smile. "You're right... I was, uh... testing you. Good job, baby girl."

She opens her gold brown eyes, looking up at my hazel eyes. "I'm doing good?"

I nod, licking my lips. "Let's do it again. Eyes closed."

She scans my face before listening.

"Now, refocus on my breath and where it's being inhaled."

She lets out a breath of air that makes her shoulder's sag.

I painfully become aware that the others have quieted down to watch and listen to us. I don't dare say anything that can turn her on. She's calm right now, and I feel it running down our bond. Stone has a bond, I know that. But Krew and Zeno haven't mated with her yet. I can tell they want to. Need is always running down our bonds. Our bond is slightly different than Esmeray's and I's are. My pack bond is a bond that we've developed over a long period of time with each other. Obviously, my twin bond with Krew is stronger but the pack bond is just as solid. Now, Esmeray and my bond is the strongest. She's my mate, alpha and packmate. I feel everything the second she feels it, and Stone seems to know when to calm her down and remind her to relax. I know she feels our bond, but I doubt it's as strong as I feel hers.

"Focus on where my breath goes. How deep it goes in my lungs, how it helps my blood pump through my veins to my heart," I whisper.

She lets out a breath of air then holds it until, finally, I think she can hear it. Her body relaxes and her bond settles. She smirks, before tapping on my knee a small beat. *My heartbeat.* I smile, trying to stay calm. "Good fucking girl," I say out of excitement.

Her eyes snap open, finding me.

Now I realize I just whispered that in a husky voice. *Oops.*

Her sweet aroma fills the air. *Yikes.* I didn't mean to turn her on. "Get your mind out of the gutter," I order.

She smirks, licking her lips and nod. "Yes, Daddy."

I roll my eyes, running a hand over my face to stop the smirk from coming on. "Calm it, Esmeray!"

Her eyes flicker down to my crotch which obviously has a boner. "Do you really want me to?"
How can she make anything and everything sexual?

"Dear god, focus!"

She throws her head back, giggling. I love the way she giggles.

Esmeray

After Kai and I trained for about an hour on my senses which happen to be going slower than I thought, it is time to move on. I mainly learned the hearing ability. I was able to tunnel focus on his heart the quickest, which after getting him aroused, made it beat faster. I noticed while doing that, everything went silent. The bugs all go silent and the distant talking ends. It makes the world around us disappear even if it's just for a quick second. For a quick second, it's just me and Kai. I barely feel the grass that surrounded us.

He did say after a while that it won't be as tunnel vision and that I will still hear the background noise as well. But for now, he said I did good.

I check my phone, texting Kira about what just happened before switching chats to see if Reed ever texted me back to apologize. As if he ever would.

"Are you okay, love?" Kai questions, moving his hand to my lower back.

I nod, closing my phone quickly before throwing it to the side. He watches me. I'm sure if he genuinely wanted to know, he can go look for himself since I don't have a passcode. But the guys are good about giving me the privacy that I deserve. Stone has gotten them in the mindset that if I want to tell them, then I will.

"So, let me look at you," Krew says, circling my body. I raise a brow, watching him. "So, you're tiny, small fisted and slow... Great." He throws his hands up. "And you can't even predict an attack if it took ten years to hit you."

"Is this supposed to be a compliment?"

He shakes his head. "Nope."

Looking at Stone, I try to do a cute pout that I doubt I succeed in. "Tell me he's lying."

Stone smirks. "Why would I lie to you?"

I roll my eyes.

"We might be able to get her to do a small, but deadly, type of fighting," Krew mutters. "Want to quickly spar to know where you stand?"

With a shrug, I say, "I don't know how to spar, but I think I can take you down."

The others give us space, but it doesn't take Krew long to pin me to the ground, bending over me. I blink. Krew is fast, faster than I thought he'd be and he's thoughtful—for the first time—with his movements.

I blink up at him.

"Did I hurt you?" he asks.

I can't even process what he did, and it is the hottest thing in the world. "No. I'm okay."

He nods, helping me to my feet. "So, you *are* slow."

I am not even pissed that I could barely get a hit on him. It turns me on more than I thought it would. This is going to take a lot of work.

Stone

My father peeks in the living room later on in the day, eyeing a sleeping Esmeray. Her head is in Zeno's lap as he rubs his fingers through her hair, and Krew gladly lets her put her feet on him as he rubs them.

I swear he might have a foot fetish.

Kai shares a small look with me before I stand and move to the foyer with my father.

"How did it go today?" he asks.

"I think it's good," I say with a nod. "She needs training every day, so let's hope the guys can come back every so often to help her. But you know how Krew's and Kai's parents are, especially after Krew's almost near death. Then Zeno's mother doesn't want him to stay often and that's a drive for him."

He nods. "When do they leave?"

"The twins leave tonight but will be back tomorrow. Zeno doesn't know yet, but she still needs to learn the basics before we teach her weapons."

"How's she doing?"

I shrug. "Doubting herself a lot more than before."

He nods, glancing back at the entrance of the doorway. "The other students died."

I let out a breath of harsh air. "Damn... Why did Esmeray and Krew survive? Is the council going to look at us further?"

He shrugs, running a hand over his face. "I'll have to talk to Brick, but I'm not sure. Everyone is confused because she's not a bad kid, besides that *smug*. But they are worried about why she survived and no one else. That, and Redman says the council has something on her dad."

I raise a brow. "Like?"

He shrugs. "Maybe you can speak to her and try to get her to say something, anything."

I look down. "It's not that simple. Esmeray tells us what she wants us to know. She can be really good at hiding things. I knew nothing about her blacking out and stuff."

"Seems like we all really don't know her."

I nod. "Fucking sucks, especially since we are mates. I should know everything."

My father pats my back. "You'll learn the more you go. Even after twenty years, your mother and I still learn things about each other. It is how the mate bond works."

Rune Hunt

I let out a sigh, running a hand through my hair. "What if she doesn't shift in time? What if they end up dying from those demonic wolves? What if—"

My father touches my chest. "Calm down before you wake her."

I take a deep breath before letting out a breath of air. "Just hard to teach someone how to be an alpha when you aren't an alpha."

He nods. "Maybe once a week I can get Brick to come down to help, along with me. But at the end of the day, no one can teach someone how to be Alpha. You just naturally are a leader and adapt to anything... Are you upset that you are not the alpha?"

I shake my head. "*Fuck*, no. I didn't want that responsibility. I would have done it if I had to, but I didn't *want* it."

My father chuckles at that response. "Good kid."

I always wanted to grow up and be like my dad but the more I got older, the quicker I realized how much work you have to put in to make everything run smoothly, and although his pack has Redmen, mine has his dumbass son who literally won't give an inch for Esmeray.

"Are you disappointed I'm not Alpha or not the only mate?"

His blue eyes meet mine. "No and no. Being Alpha is the hardest and most stressful thing I've ever done. I would rather it be on anyone else but you.

119

You'd at least be able to handle it, but Reed would never." I nod with him. "And if Esmeray's wolf wants more guys, I don't think that's horrible. It could be because it seems like she had no one in her life and now she has five mates."

I nod. "If Reed can get his head out of his ass."

My father nods. "Agreed. Now get to bed. Time for a new day."

Esmeray

Rolling over, my fingers graze a bare chest. *Mhm.* I run a finger down the chest, to the nipples that perk under my touch, and then further down to this person's abs. From there, I run a palm over the abs.

From the cooling mint smell, I can tell it's Stone.

He puts his hand over mine, making me open my eyes and look up. His eyes are still closed, and his chest rises and falls slowly. We are in a bed that isn't mine, which makes me look around.

It's his room, I'm assuming. It's filled with decor and shelves full of stuff. I sit up, taking in the row of snowboards and the row of skateboards on his wall. Then on the same wall as his television, there are game systems with the action figures of the games surrounding it. On another wall are movie scripts in cases, and posters of drawings of hot women from games and movies.

I smirk. *He's like a typical man.*

"Yeah, I figured you could sleep in my bed once," Stone mutters, curling up so his lips touch my back.

I look back to the snowboards. "Do you snowboard?"

He hums. "Dad takes us with his pack sometimes. I used to snowboard in high school as well."

"I've never been," I mutter.

"Maybe we can go."

"Do you actually skateboard?"

He nods. "Well... longboard. Krew got me into it when we went on vacation to California once."

I look over at him. "My dad used to take me to the skatepark to rollerblade and skateboard. It was cool."

His eyes finally open and move to meet my eyes. My face is dangerously close to his, our foreheads almost touching. "What's your favorite movie?"

I smile, not expecting it. "Uh... I have a lot. Favorite horror is Saw."

"Any?"

"I love guts. I love zombie movies, too. George A. Romero is the best director of all time."

Stone rolls his eyes at me. "Quintan Tarantino is *by far* the greatest."

I huff. "No. Fuck off."

"He made *Pulp Fiction*!"

"I've never seen it! I don't want to."

Stone gasps, wide eyed. "You take that back."

I raise a brow, trying not to smirk. "No!"

He gasps again, turning away. "I can't do this anymore. I don't want this relationship."

Rolling my eyes, I kick off the blankets to crawl over him. "Is that where the scripts are from?"

He nods. "All signed. Do you like *Resident Evil*?"

"The movies and books are so good!"

He shakes his head. "The games."

"I hate horror games."

His brows pull together.

I shrug. "I get too scared."

He bursts out laughing at me, making me cross my arms over my chest. "But you'll watch horror movies?!"

"I don't get scared!" I giggle.

He buries his face into my neck, laughing. "If we... if we play together, will you be less scared?"

I raise a brow. "Why can't we play like... *Mario* or something?"

That makes him laugh hard. "You're a fucking scaredy cat."

I try to push him away as I stick out my bottom lip. "No!"

"Yes!" He pulls me back, kissing my lips. "It's okay, baby. I'll protect you."

My heart melts. "Whatever."

"Favorite singer or band?"

I raise a brow. "Are we playing twenty questions again? Why do you keep asking me questions?"

"Two questions, Esme. You get one."

I smirk, biting my lip. "Why are you questioning me?"

His face softens. "I feel like we don't know each other like I thought we did."

That makes my breath soften. Here I am, being an ass. "I like Fall Out Boy or Three Days Grace."

"I like Seether and a few other rock ones."

I nod. "I like them. Do you like to Bring Me the Horizon?"

He nods. "Oh, so you're into emo screamo?"

I snort. "No!"

"It's okay, you can tell me!"

I push him away, but he pulls me close. I move closer, placing my lips near his. "Favorite food."

"Steak is good. Anything with steak makes me happy. Birthday gift idea, you naked with a steak on your body."

I snort. "I like Chinese food. Favorite drink?"

He yawns. "Coffee. You?"

"Red Bull or hot chocolate."

I nod as his phone goes off. His hand reaches behind me and grasps the phone.

"Hello?" His smile fades. "Yes, Krew. We are up... No, my cock is not buried in her. It's about to be."

I let out a laugh, pushing away from him.

"Jealous?... No? You sound it... Bye, asshole." He hangs up on Krew.

"Did they leave?" I question. I did remember falling asleep on Zeno, then waking up to Stone carrying me to the bedroom. But I insisted on getting kisses from everyone before I went to bed.

He nods. "Kai will be with us today. Krew's mom wanted to go out with him for lunch and have a day with him."

I nod. "Zeno?"

"He's gonna try to make it. His mom happens to be stricter than most."

I nod again. "That's okay. We can still have a good day."

He smiles at me. "Damn straight, baby." He leans in, kissing my lips. I enjoy his kisses even with the morning breath. He doesn't seem to care about mine at all.

I pull back, smirking up at him. "So, about that cock being buried inside of me?"

Rejected Wolf

He chuckles but moves away.

Today is apparently leg day. I'm not as sore as I thought I was going to be, but Krew did say I would heal fast. While doing cardio on the bike, I ask Kai if I will get a booty the size of his if I squat enough. He laughs at my joke.

Kai's butt isn't tiny. It's rounder than mine, even if my hips are slightly bigger than his. Stone and Zeno for sure have the biggest ass. They are just perfectly round, probably bigger than mine, even in these tight grey leggings.

A few minutes after we finish with cardio, I step off, moving to the mirror and take a picture of my ass. Kai and I meet eyes in the long mirror that reflect to the whole gym. I smirk, and say, "Progress photos. I want a nice ass if I'm forced to work out."

He shakes his head, taking a sip of water.

I send the picture to Zeno and Krew, sweaty ass and all.

Krew texts back instantly.

Krew: I'm not there to see that.

I glance at Stone, who is setting up his speaker.

Me: I know, you are missing out on some booty workouts today.

Krew: Are you saying my ass isn't fat?

I snort.

Me: Yes.

Zeno finally texts back.

126

Zeno: Fuck. Don't do this to me, Mami.

Me: Wouldn't you just rather be between them?

Zeno: Don't tempt me, princesa.

I bit my lip, just as Stone snatches my phone. "No flirting," he grumbles.

I gasp. "And that's exactly why I didn't send you the ass picture."

He opens my phone and probably instantly sees the conversation between Zeno and me, which I changed his name in my phone to "Z" with black hearts. Stone has white hearts, Krew has yellow, and Kai has blue. I watch his smirk as he starts to type something.

"Hey!" I reach for it, having him lift it in the air. I try to reach for it again, but apparently, he's like a jolly green *fucking* giant with long ass arms. I grab his bicep, trying to pull him down, but no matter how much of my weight I put into it, he doesn't bulge until he sends the message and slips the phone onto one of the tall shelves. "Stone!"

He looks at me, like he's fucking innocent. "Yes, baby?"

I look at Kai for help, which he offers none. "Are you just gonna let him bully me?!"

Kai smiles. "He's *your* boyfriend."

I roll my eyes, moving to Kai. "So are you. Can you reach it, baby?"

Rejected Wolf

Kai raises a brow, looking at Stone. "No. Let's get to work."

I cross my arm, pouting. "I'm unloved…"

Stone snorts because it is far from the truth. His heavy hand slaps my ass, making me yelp and jump away. "Time to get to work on that ass, Esmeray. Can't disappoint your men."

My eyes roll again. "You'd still love me if I was a pancake."

Kai nods in thought. "I do like pancakes."

Stone works me to the fullest, making me squat my max with high reps—which isn't a lot. We jam out to music, which I like most of the songs. And he did everything in his power to fucking kill my thighs. It works, by the end, I'm a sweating, jelly mess.

I collapse on the mat in the corner, loving the cool feeling of it. Kai crouches beside me, handing me a cold bottle of water. That had to be my third one today. Apparently, it's good to pee every five fucking seconds. Kai wants me to try to drink a gallon a day of water alone. I think he would love to see me fucking drown.

"Are you okay?" Kai asks, pulling my messy hair back and sticking it in my hair tie for me.

"I'm unloved and dead."

Kai sits by me. He looks just as exhausted as I feel, but he's stronger than I am. "Are you ready for more mind things today?"

I roll over, looking up. "Born ready."

I lie. I am not ready, but I don't want to let him know that. I do worse today than I did yesterday. I can't hear his heart no matter how much I try, plus a headache is making it worse. Kai still kissed my head and tells me I did good. He's too sweet to me. I rub his lower back a bit before he leaves, because I know he hurt it when he was lifting.

He might not be back tomorrow so he can rest.

Stone runs me a bath before going to take a shower in his room. Finally, he gives me back my phone. He sent Zeno a message that said, "When are you going to fuck me, Daddy? When are you going to let Stone and you both fuck me?"

He texted back.

Zeno: Tell Esmeray to call me back when you aren't training.

He knew it wasn't me.

I dial him up, putting him on speaker as I text Krew that I finished for the day.

"If this isn't Esmeray, I don't want to speak," Zeno's deep, raspy voice says as soon as he picks up.

"It's me, mi amor." I sigh as I sink into the water. "Were you sleeping?"

"No, just laying down, bored."

"Yeah? Stone took my phone. Apparently, you're a distraction."

He chuckles. It's heavy and runs straight to my aching core. "I knew I shouldn't have sent you that picture of my elbows."

I snort. "Oh, yeah! That set me off."

"I know it did. Very easy to turn you on."

I roll my eyes. "I'll have you know; it is not. I just happen to always be turned on."

"Are you turned on right now?" he asks huskily.

As if my pussy has a mind of its own, it throbs and the coils in my stomach begin turning. I swallow. "No." He chuckles. The deepness running down my spine. "Stop it. It takes me a long time to get turned on."

"Sure, Mami." His Hispanic accent just hit the right spot on my pussy to make my thighs clam close. "What do you need to get turned on? Do you touch yourself? Dick picture? Video?"

My jaw drops. "Z!"

"Tell me, mamcita. If I could leave right now, I'd be fucking you where you stand, but I can't. I want to hear you come for me."

"Oh my god…" I bit my lip a bit nervous. "A video wouldn't hurt." I hear him shift. "If you want. If you're not busy."

"Never be too busy for you," he mutters, shifting. He grunts, telling me he just fisted his cock. I rub my thighs together, whimpering to relieve the aching. He moans as I guess he begins rubbing himself. Then he says, "Check your phone."

I twist around, water splashing around me as I pick up my phone.

"Are you in the bath?"

"Yes." Smirking, I open his video, seeing his long, girthy veiny cock in his ringed fingers. "Oh, fuck." His hands run up and down his long length, making my thighs tighten again. "Oh…" Then the video ends.

"You like, baby?"

I bit my lip. "Mhm." I point the phone camera at myself, taking a video of me rubbing bubbles into my heavy breast before my hand drops to my pussy. I finger my clit slightly, earning a slight buck and moan. "How did you manage to get me so horny?"

He chuckles, and I sent him the video back.

"Check your phone," I say, sitting back down and still rubbing my clit.

"Jesus, Esmeray!"

The way he said my name makes me enter a finger into myself. "Fuck," I pant.

"Keep playing with yourself," Zeno says. "I want to hear you come for me."

I lick my lips. "Are you playing with yourself?"

"Of course, baby."

The thought of Zeno rubbing himself makes my heels press into the bottom of the tub. "Fuck, I wish you were inside of me."

"I want to taste you so bad, Esmeray."

My hips begin to buck as my toes begin to tingle. "I'm not—I'm not gonna last, Zeno!"

Rejected Wolf

He moans, almost sending me over the edge. "Me either, baby. I'm just staring at your beautiful breasts."

I drop my head back, closing my eyes. Stars dance behind my eyes as I rub my clit faster and faster until I'm crying out over and over. My legs shake violently as I moan his name.

"Come for me, baby. Come for Papi."

I stiffen, crying out and moaning as a wave of pleasure crashes into me.

He moans and grunts until he finally lets out a large growl of his release. "Good fucking girl."

I twitch, settling back into the water. "I want you soon, Zeno."

"Soon, baby."

Esmeray

All throughout August, I have been ignored by Reed, I tried to text him more and talk to him more but not once did he come see me.

I hated how weak I felt doing it, and it was even worse when he left me on read.

Zeno and I never got around to actually having sex. He visited to help me and, on my days off, he hangs out with me, but we didn't get a chance to be alone because he left every night.

Krew and Kai came to visit and help when they can, Kai more than Krew. Krew still texted me, flirted with me, and even kissed me when he left.

Rejected Wolf

Stone is always here, which I haven't gotten tired of. I love being around him and even better getting to know them all. My bond with him has grown a lot, and we can even state each other's favorite things without much thought.

But something feel… like I am incomplete.

Maybe that is Reed's fault.

The headaches have gotten worse to the point that I went to the doctors with Kira to get a higher dose of painkillers. The chest pains have me stopping to take breaks during trainings, even though I can tell I'm getting stronger and faster. My reaction speed is faster, and my body is getting more tone.

Working out and training has become routine and a distraction. It helps me work off the week's stress while also feeling good.

My mind still wanders to the guy in court and why his face was so familiar, but I can't pinpoint it and it's always on the tip of my tongue.

The dream from my coma always comes to me here and there, but I can't remember that either.

On the days I'm off, they're the worst until I see Stone or the others. They make me happy, but the constant aching won't go away. I wonder if Stone feels it and if he'll say anything.

"Let's go for a run," Stone says. I glance at the treadmill. "No, no, outside in the woods."

I nod. "Sure."

Stone takes off his band from his waist that he uses to keep his body stiff when he squats. Then he kicks off his shoes and socks. His hands go to his waistband before I stop him.

"What type of run is this?" I raise a brow with a smirk.

"You're gonna chase me while I'm a wolf."

I blink. "But aren't you ten times stronger and faster?"

He shrugs, dropping his pants and letting his cock be free. I've seen his dick at least a thousand times, yet my stomach still coils with lust and heat. "Get the door."

Then he shifts. I watch each bone break and deconstruct and reconstruct. I hear each one until I see the fur rise against his skin, and then he's on all fours, a white wolf.

He blinks up at me.

They've all shifted in front of me, yet I'm still amazed.

Like a fucking child, I reach down and touch his fur. It feels soft and amazing under my fingers. He even closes his eyes and leans into it.

"Do you want belly rubs? I can ask you who is a good boy!" I tease.

His blue eyes open and look at me. With a growl, he thinks, *No.*

"Awe, come on. Who's a good boy?"

Rejected Wolf

He snaps at my fingers but gives me enough time to pull back.

"Well, obviously, it's not you," I mutter, moving to the door and opening it to the side yard. Stone trots outside, shaking out his fur, and parts of me are jealous of him and wants that.

I want to know what it feels like to fully shift. Kai said I should have started feeling my wolf at any point, especially when I've begun getting in tune with my senses.

But I don't feel her...

Stone looks back at me. *Ready?*

I inhale deeply, singling out all the animals around me. Birds flap their wings against the morning breeze while crickets run and hide. Spiders crinkle as they crawl over their webs, waiting for the buzzing flies to join them. The breeze runs over me, carrying the scent of a burned-out campfire from last night and the morning dew. I open my eyes, nodding before taking off after Stone.

I'm faster than I've ever been, even if it's not as fast as Stone's wolf. My thicker thighs carry me the distance of the run, hiking higher and higher up the hill.

Stone looks back at me, making me smile. He knows I'm not going to catch him this way, but still; we enjoy the chase. My mind races as we do, unable to stop thinking about Reed and how much fun we all could have together.

Rune Hunt

My head spins once we cease movement at the cliff after fifteen minutes. I reach up, taking hold of my thumping head. The world around me goes black for a second and spins.

"Esmeray." Stone's voice brings me back to reality.

I'm still dizzy, but it's not because of the height or what we just ran. I'm barely out of breath from it.

His hands cup my cheek, and he tilts my head back. He's in human form now, and I barely heard him shift back. "Are you okay? You were wavering."

I blink. "Was I?"

He touches my forehead. "Are you too hot or too tired?"

I shake my head. "No. No. I'm okay."

"You looked like you were going to pass out."

I shake my head again. "No. I'm okay, Stone."

His eyes scan my face, obviously really believing me. "You are taking the weekend off."

My brows pull together. "No! We have one and a half months left and—"

He moves away from me. "I'm telling you: you aren't working this weekend. You're exhausted and overworked."

My brows pull together. "And how do you know that?!"

"I feel it."

I roll my eyes, crossing my arms as I watch him walk towards where we came from. "Who made you Alpha?"

He barely turns around. "Esmeray, drop it."

"I haven't shifted yet!"

"And you won't if you are burned out. Let's go back."

I stare after him. "No."

He stops, looking over his shoulder at me. "No?"

"No. I think you forgot you are not the alpha and I make the decisions. I want to train. I want to shift. I want to be able to go back to school so we can all be together again because…" *I miss my guys.* I swallow, eyes prickling. "We train like normal. I won't pass out. I'm not tired."

Stone turns around. "Do you not care about yourself? Do you not care that you almost passed out on a cliff, and I had to catch you from falling?"

My brows pull together. "No, you didn't."

He raises a brow. "Are you calling me a liar?"

I close my mouth, just looking at him.

"Let's at least go back for breakfast, *Alpha.*"

I roll my eyes, pushing past him. "Shift back, so I don't have to look at you because I'm mad at you."

Stone let out a snort. "Yes, *Alpha.*"

Fucker.

Rune Hunt

It's hard being mad at Stone, especially when he is looking out for me, but I ignore him through lifting and breakfast, until I go by the pool for my training, and wait for Kai.

Does he know what's at stake? We can all be kicked out of Moon Born because I can't figure out how to shift. I've tried so many times with Zeno, but not once, did I get it right.

I throw myself on the grass.

I'm useless. Reed was right. This is all my fault. Krew almost died, all those student's deaths, and even us about to be kicked out. Can I do anything right?

Please, please, Miss. Wolf inside of me, come out. I don't even care if you want to eat a bird, Krew has done it. Do you want a bird? I can get you one.

Silence.

Tears sting my eyes. I can't even focus. I sit up, pulling my knees up under my chin. Stone was only looking out for me, and I started a fight, like an asshole.

Am I really tired and trying to hide it from myself? I want to push myself. I want to be Alpha, even if my wolf is failing me.

Yet... I feel so alone.

Reed's rejected words replay in my head at night, disturbing my dreams. And it makes me feel like my guys might feel the same way. Of course, I'm so weak. I let him in my head. I try my hardest to ignore his words or to text him to take it back, but of course, he ignores me.

On my weakest days, I beg him to let me talk to him. On my better days, I ignore him.

I am a rejected wolf. Whether that dream is real or not, I am feeling rejected now.

Well, a rejected non-wolf. I can't be a part of the furries if I can't shift. And I so badly want to be a part of them.

Goosebumps rise against my skin, and the hair on my body stands up. Someone is behind me. I hear something crinkle behind me and feel the air as someone reaches out for me quickly.

I move fast, twisting and grabbing the hand. In a swift movement, the person twists me and pins me to the ground. Heat is pressed right between my legs with a familiar scent that I love. A boyish grin lights up his face.

"Better, I guess," Krew mutters. Slowly his smile fades, and his hazel eyes meet mine. "What's wrong—"

Before he can finish, I lift my hips, twisting hard. In a swift movement, I gain control, sitting on his chest and pinning his arms down with my knees. Hair and grass fall in my face, hanging down towards him.

He smirks. "Damn. Is this my hello?" His eyes move to my crotch, that sits dangerously close to his chin. I smirk down at him.

"Hi," I mutter.

Rune Hunt

"Hi, baby." His eyes soften, making me melt.

"I want a hello like this." A deep velvety voice comes from behind me. I twist around to see my dark-haired boy.

"Zeno!" I jump to my feet and rush to him. Before he can even process, I'm jumping on him. I haven't seen either of them in a week or two, and never together.

Zeno and I land together on the grass with a small thud. He wraps his arms around me, laughing. "Hi."

I grab his stubbly jaw and crash my lips into his. He reaches up, pushing my hair behind my ear. He tastes like coffee, which normally is gross, but my men taste so good when they drink coffee. I can tell what each of them likes in theirs. Zeno likes his black, and his lips taste bitter because of it.

"Hey, Mami," He pulls back.

I smile. "Hi."

"I never got a kiss!" Krew whines, making me get off of Zeno. I move to Krew, pulling him close before almost kissing him.

He waits for me but of course, I pull away, glancing over. "Hi, Kai!" I felt Kai in the doorway of the backdoor, stronger than I ever have before.

Krew groans.

"Don't let me interrupt, but don't forget about me after," Kai says, leaning against the door.

Rejected Wolf

Krew gets impatient, pulling my jaw to crash his lips into mine. I almost fucking moan, causing my stomach to ignite. We kiss like we've never kissed before. My hand fists his shirt at his hips as his hand cradles my face. And when he pulls back, he nods, "Yeah, that's better. Now, go to your little boyfriend."

As much as I love tempting Krew, him and Zeno have been the hugest *desire* in my life. I crave to kiss them, to hold them and fuck them.

But I listen.

I move away. Kai pulls me into a hug and kisses my lips so sweetly.

"What are you guys doing here?" I question, looking up through my lashes.

"You don't want to see us?" he says with a chuckle.

I shake my head. "But all at once?"

"I asked them to stay for the weekend." Stone's voice comes from the foyer as he moves to us.

I meet his eyes.

"I figured you might be missing them," he says.

I let out a huff, moving to wrap my arms around him. He didn't deserve my attitude. "Sorry, I'm an ass."

He shakes his head. "I overstepped. I'm sorry."

"No, you didn't. You were worried," I mutter.

He kisses my head.

142

He was right, holding me like this made me feel like I was exhausted and could sleep. But do I have to tell him that? I let out a sigh, pulling back and looking down. "You were right."

"I'm sorry. What was that?" he teases.

I push him. "You heard me."

"No, I didn't." A smirk curls on his lips.

I roll my eyes. "Someone lift me up so he can hear me."

Zeno listens, holding me up by my waist.

But face to face, I just smile. "I don't want to hear anyone say I'm short ever again!"

Zeno drops me with a laugh.

I rub my hands together. "What are we doing today?"

Esmeray

Our first night together feels short. We all sits around, talking, and watching movies. Stone orders us pizza, although I don't feel hungry anymore.

I twist in bed the next morning, sandwiched between Krew and Kai. *Mhm… Twin sandwich, yes please.* Sitting up slightly, I glance around to look for Zeno and Stone, but they are not in bed with us or in my room. My hand runs up Krew's bare chest as I push my ass right into Kai's crotch. Both already have a hard-on from the morning.

Krew's eyes flutter open, just as I run my hand over his abs. "What a good way to wake up."

I smirk. "Sandwiched between twins?"

Kai kisses my shoulder a few times before nuzzling his nose into my skin. His warmth covers my back as he shifts closer.

"Mhm," Krew says, grabbing my neck before pulling my lips into his. Krew kisses like a god and I almost melt right into his hands. I'm laying down and I'm still weak in my knees.

Our lips move together as he pulls me flush against him to press his hard dick into my hips. Softly, I moan into his mouth and that makes Kai do the same, dick digging right into my ass.

Twins... at once? Yes. Please.

Kai's hands run over my stomach, fingers brushing my ribs. Krew's fingers wrap around my neck and jaw, tightening lightly. I think he thinks I would twist away and give him blue balls. *Never. I'd never give myself blue balls for the sake of teasing.*

Heat boils in my stomach as Kai finally cups my breast. Arching and moaning, my nails dig into Krew's shoulder. I begin grinding on them, my pussy running along Krew's length as Kai gets my ass.

Krew lets go off my neck to rip off my tank top, grabbing my bare breasts just as Kai lets them go. Within seconds, Krew's hot wet mouth is over them.

I drop my head back, arching to get more.

Kai grabs my jaw and twists my body, so I'm on my back and he can finally kiss me sweetly, yet so feverishly.

Rejected Wolf

Someone's—*Krew's*—fingers rub my pussy from the outside of my shorts, causing me to gasp. I run my hand down Kai's chest and feel for his dick as Krew's fingers enter my shorts. If Krew's fingers are anything like his mouth, I need that.

I lift my hips, urging him further as I rub Kai's dick, the way he likes.

Just as Krew's index finger touches my clit and his tongue flicks my hard nipple, the door opens, causing us all to pull back. We knew at least it wasn't Silver or Liza, because they would have knocked.

Zeno chuckles. "Really?"

I peek over Krew at him. "Why did you interrupt?"

He raises a brow. "You have stuff to do today."

I huff. Honestly, I didn't want to work out and I thought Stone said I didn't have to. I roll onto Krew, pressing my chest into his. I glance at Zeno's watching eyes as I lean down, peppering kisses against Krew's neck, feeling his pulse, and then up his jaw.

Krew let out a sigh, grabbing my shoulders. "I hate to fucking do this, but we have to get up."

I pull back with a gasp. "What? No!"

Krew nods. "I can survive another day, but you have plans."

"That I have no idea what they're about and I'm sure it can wait an extra five minutes. I promise, you both won't last long."

146

Krew snorts.

"Up in five. You have reservations," Zeno says, walking out.

I sit up. "Huh?"

Krew's eyes take in my breasts before he sits up. "You and I are going out."

Looking down at him, I almost want to forget the plans and go back to what we were just doing. "When?"

"For brunch."

I glance over at Kai. "Like a date, *date*?"

Krew smirks. "Mhm. We decided I'd be the first to take you out on an actual date."

My chest jumps with excitement. I almost forgot about the best threesome I was ever going to have. "What do I wear?!"

"I'll pick you out some clothes. Go get into the shower," he mutters, kissing my chest.

Glancing between both of them, I decide I want a date a bit more. Only like an inch more. "This is not over. I will have you both at once."

Kai makes a noise before chuckling.

But as soon as I step off the bed, I drop my shorts seductively before moving to the bathroom.

Krew groans and I hear the bed groan when he throws himself back down. "I can't stand you, Esmeray."

"Oops."

I close the door behind me. I take my time

showering and in only a towel, I go back into my room. It's empty of hot men, and the bed is made, and the clothes picked up. *How sweet. I did miss them for sure.*

On the bed, the clothes that Krew picked out are laid out. They are a black deep V neck, exposed shoulders top, and white jeans with a few rips to match. He even picked black boots that Stone brought me to match.

Krew knows what he wants.

I get dressed, struggling to get the pants past my thick thighs. *Oh, shit… is it muscle or fat that my birth control caused?* Looking in the mirror, I realize my ass did get rounder and if these pants fit, Krew might want to take me right here. I wish…

I picked slightly bigger black jeans. Although it says the same size, no jeans are really the same size. I grab a matching purse with a gold chain after fixing my hair to hang down and cover my shoulders. The white strain is pushed behind my ear. I clank my way down the stairs, feeling powerful with each step.

Voice come from the living room, and I twist to peek inside. All the guys are lounging around, talking to Silver.

Krew turns, making me realize we are wearing matching clothes or *were*. He's wearing white pants and I'm not. Yet, he whistles, drawing the attention of the others.

"Damn…" Stone mutters. "Never mind, Krew, I'll take her on a date first."

Zeno agrees, nodding while Kai smiles at me.

"Wait. What happened to the white pants?" Krew asks, standing.

"They didn't fit. I've gained some… muscle," I say with a shrug, wanting to run back upstairs to find matching jeans to match him. *Man, I ruined this.*

"You have a fat ass," Stone says with a smile.

Silver slaps his head, scowling him. I bite back a smile.

"Sorry, sorry. *Respectfully*, you have a fat ass."

I snort, grabbing Krew's shoulder not to fall over from laughing. "Jesus!"

Krew wraps his arm around my back, still taller than me. "Say goodbye to the idiots."

I smile, holding open my arm for hugs. Zeno is the first, kissing my lips softly to not mess up my lipstick before hugging me.

"Have fun, but not too much," he says in my ear.

Kai is next and he kisses my jaw. "Don't let Krew be an asshole to you."

I snort. *He would never.*

Stone is last, grabbing my ass and pulling me into a hard kiss. I giggle against him, pushing him away, glancing at Silver who ignores us to talk to Zeno. "Oh, sorry. *Respectfully*," Stone says with a chuckle and kissing me once more.

149

I roll my eyes, pulling back. "Did you mess up my lipstick?"

"No. But I can..."

I hit his chest.

"Yeah, yeah. Have fun, E."

Smiling up at him, I wonder if a part of him is jealous we haven't been able to go on a date yet, but I think he knows he'll get his chance.

We both say bye to everyone before stepping towards Krew's shiny 1981 Camaro. He opens the door for me and then rounds the car to get in. I half thought he'd slide across the hood. *But this is Krew's baby.* His grandfather gave it to him before he died, Kai told me that much.

"Sorry, we don't match anymore. That was my old white pair," I say when he starts up the car.

He chuckles, peeling from the parking lot. "It's okay. I just thought you'd like to match."

I smile. *I did.* He looks so handsome in his black t-shirt and his white slacks. His hair is done, letting brown curls to fall against his forehead. A smirk is on his lips as he places his hand on my thigh. *Mhm, I want to taste him in the worst kind of way.* "Where are we going? How far away is it?"

"Forty minutes," he says with a shrug.

"Good, we have time." I shift, rubbing his crotch until his dick grows right in my hand.

"Dear god," he hisses as my fingers rub him.

150

Rune Hunt

I chuckle, unbuckling his pants and unzipping them. "Do you think you can handle it?"

"Yes." He nods so quickly. His eyes never move from the road. "I'll tell you right fucking now, it's been a while and I'm going to come quick."

"That's if I let you..." I tease, freeing his cock. It springs upward. I've seen the outline of his dick before and each time, he's really hard. The veins run straight to his tip. It probably has been a while.

I lean over the middle console, ducking under his arm as he gets on the highway. I lick his tip so softly. His hips jerk and he hisses.

Goal: to suck his dick better than anyone else ever could.

I fist his shaft, running my tongue up the side to kiss the tip. My lipstick leaves a mark.

"Don't you dare tease me." His hand runs down my back, moving my hair to one side.

I giggle, kissing him again then taking him into my mouth.

He moans, hips rising.

But I'm in control. I pull back, seeing red streaks from my lipstick. *Fuck. That's hot. I wish I wasn't wearing jeans because I want to touch myself.*

I take him back in my mouth, hollowing my cheeks and slowly bobbing my head as my tongue swirls.

His free hand smacks my ass.

Rejected Wolf

I hum, sucking his dick. I find what he likes very easily. He likes when my tongue licks his balls as he's deep into my mouth, and when my tongue teases his tip. After a few minutes of him moaning and groaning and trying to shove my head down, he hisses, "I'm gonna come. Don't stop."

I thought about it, stopping for a half second, but his words make my body tingle.

"No. No. Please, don't stop. I need to come, Esmeray. Please, baby." He begs. "Please, make me come."

So, I bob faster, wanting to taste him and give him the release I made him wait for.

His free hand grips my hair as he moans nonstop and thrusts into my mouth. Finally, he stiffens, twitching as cum runs down my throat. I swallow, sucking up some drool.

"Jesus!" He gasps, leaning back. "Fuck, that was good."

I lap up the drool and left over cum before pulling back. I reach into my purse, using tissues to clean both of us up before he puts his dick away, sadly. "Was it good?"

He smirks. "You know damn well it was good. And next time, you won't be in charge."

I scoff, using my mirror to reapply my lipstick and fix my curls.

His hand sneaks around my neck and pulls me close to him. "I'm going to fuck your throat and make you fucking beg for me. Then I will fuck you until you're screaming, got it?"

I bit my lip, pussy throbbing for that right now. "Yes. I got it."

"Yes, what?" His eyes are on the road, but the dominance makes me cower a bit even as he tightens his fist.

"Daddy," I breath out.

"Good girl. Now, let's go and actually eat," he says, letting me go. Krew is two different people sometimes. He's so funny and goofy, but during sex, I can tell he's going to dominate me. His tattooed hand holds my thigh the rest of the way as we talk about nothing important.

Krew

Esmeray looks so *fucking* gorgeous today, even if she's not wearing those pants I picked out. I would be lying if I say I'm not nervous. First time, I was nervous on a date, but she doesn't feel what I feel. *Thank god.*

Our bond will be tied after sex.

She giggles about something her, and Stone joked about while training. I'm slightly jealous she lives with him, but I'm grateful, it's him. He took care of her and even called us yesterday to come together for the weekend.

He said he noticed that although she acts the same, he can tell she's off. Like she's been sad, even though she smiles. She's always tired and Kira says she complains about headaches all the time and takes her to get migraine medicine, but it doesn't work. She's on birth control now, so she's not pregnant.

The only thing I can think of is Reed and the distance between them is getting to her. He doesn't really talk to me much anymore and I refuse to give in to his delusions anymore. Reed might be ignoring her too which makes her upset. Then my mother put me in a bubble for a bit and didn't let me come out as often as Kai. She texts me five times a day, wondering how I am.

I understand. I almost died.

Would that have hurt Esmeray more? I'm sure it would. Silver says losing a mate always hurts because they are a part of you.

She has five parts of her.

I need to talk to Reed soon to see if he can come to even just see us. But his pride is too big and won't let him say he's sorry.

He really wanted to be alpha, even hated Stone sometimes for it. Zeno told me Reed always complained that they were waiting too long to figure it out and that he deserved to be the alpha, not Stone.

You can't even talk to your pack, even if it's just to catch up with us. Why would you be a better alpha than Stone or Esmeray?

In a few months, school starts back again, and he hasn't helped with anything. Esmeray is nowhere near shifting as if something is holding her back. In my opinion, she should just *fucking* reject him and lose the weight of him dragging her down.

She's too fucking sweet for her own good.

I pull up to the restaurant and see Esmeray dancing. Dancing for food.

I smirk. "Ready, baby girl?"

She nods. "Yes!" I get out, round the car and open the door for her before the valet could even touch the door. She fixes her hair, looking as beautiful as ever. I hand over the keys to the guy.

"Hello, Mr. Traux."

I nod at the kid. I don't know his name because he's new. I hook my arm around Esmeray's, and lead her up the steps to the nice little country club for the rich.

"Bring girls here a lot to impress them?" she teases.

Nice try. "No, my father owns the place." She makes an "oh" face. "And you're the first woman I've ever brought here." She smirks, looking down at her shoes.

I haven't been on many dates, even though my reputation has me with a lot of girls. I figured I wouldn't have a mate like the guys. None of us found ours around the same time as other wolves did. Now I see why.

"Table for two, Mr. Traux?"

"Yes, please."

The hostess leads us to our table, a bit secluded from the others. I help Esmeray sit and push her in before sitting.

"Wait, what is this place?" she asks with a smile.

"A country club for the rich wolves," I explain. "There's boring golf, a pool here, and other stuff."

She nods. "Must be nice having money like that to afford a membership."

I nod. "Yeah. But the food is really fucking good."

She looks down at the menu.

My tongue runs over my lips, eyes glue to her. "Are you ever... sad, that we have a lot of money?"

She glances up, chuckling. "No. Fuck, no. I just don't want you guys paying for everything forever, and I don't want you guys to think I'm using you." She leans forward. "Maybe your dad will let me wash dishes for money."

I roll my eyes. "Yeah. No. My girl's not working."

She cocks a brow. "What?"

"Get a fucking hobby. Make sweaters, but you don't have to work. I rather work with my dad, painfully, than to see you waiting on people, hands and knees."

"Again," she adds.

Rejected Wolf

I nod. "Again. We have enough money for you, so don't be shy and take our blessings. You rarely ask for anything."

She shrugs. "I don't need anything. You guys talk to me, and I have food and a stable roof over my head. I'm happy even without all these gifts."

A smirk runs across my lips. I swear I can buy Esmeray a drink from the corner store and she'll be so happy. Reed doesn't know what he's talking about. "I know, but I like to spoil you, to be honest. Stone does too."

She nods. "Yeah, he does. He bought me another wardrobe because the cops wouldn't let us go back for our clothes. Insane."

I nod. "Do you miss working? Do you miss your apartment or anything?"

She shrugs. "It's not like I had stuff that would make me go back. My clothes were only work clothes. I had a few crystals I liked, but they were tiny and cheap. Even my books were from the dollar store. I had nothing. No movies because of streaming online. No pictures because of a fire that happened when I was smaller. I…" She shrugs. "I was surviving."

Before I can speak, the waitress comes over. "Good morning, I'm Sailor. Anything to drink?"

"Two mimosas and two waters," I order, watching Esmeray's face I could tell I made a good choice. "And a few more minutes with the menu, please."

Rune Hunt

She nods, moving away.

I rub my forehead, trying to remember where we were in our conversation. "Do you feel... like you're still trying to survive?"

She shakes her head. "I used to live from paycheck to paycheck. I'm so grateful I don't have to do that anymore. I hate that it's at the expense of you guys but... you guys don't seem to mind."

I shrug. *Let me not tell her about my allowance that I get once a month.* "I actually have been working."

"Really? Here?"

Shaking my head, I ignore the glint in her eyes. She seems to like working men. "Zeno's brother has been letting me help in his shop."

"His car shop?"

She rests her chin in the palm of her hand and looks up at me with those huge chocolate eyes. Makes me wonder how good she'd look on her knees, eyes watering. I shift, trying to calm my growing dick.

"You like doing that? Working on cars?"

Nodding, I clear my throat. "It's the only thing I can actually retain information of. I feel good when I can fix anything. School has never been my thing."

She smiles. "Wow, that's amazing. Maybe one day you can have a shop."

I return the smile. That's the dream. "What are you in the mood to eat?" She looks down at the menu.

159

"I know what I'm in the mood to eat…" Her face heats up, turning red. She knew what I meant.

"Believe it or not, I hate breakfast food besides French toast."

"Their French toast is good, not as good as Stone's, but good. I would recommend the surf and turf, just because steak is the best thing I've ever had."

She rolls her eyes. "Men and their steak."

Sailor is back, setting down our drinks. "Are you ready to order?" She's looking more at me, flirty glints in her eyes.

"Order first, baby," I say to Esmeray, seeing her biting the inside of her cheek with jealousy.

"Just the surf and turf," she answers.

"How would you like your steak?"

"Medium."

"Same thing. But bring the charcuterie board as an appetizer."

"Yes, sir." She gives me a flirtatious look before moving away.

I scrunch my face before taking a sip of my drink.

"I can fight," Esmeray says, making me almost spit what is in my mouth.

"No. Down girl." She smiles at me. "But I can have them switch waitresses."

"No. Maybe she's flirting for a bigger tip. I used to do it all the time."

I blink. "With people on an obvious date?"

She sighs. "No. But just keep calling me baby and maybe she'll catch the hint. It's fine. I'm surprised you didn't notice she was staring when you ordered our drinks."

Because I'm only focused on you. My tongue wets my lips just as I feel a familiar aura coming our way. I push out my chair and stand and turn just as my father arrives at our table. "Hey, Dad."

He hugs me, patting my back.

Esmeray stands, and he hugs her. "You look very pretty, Esmeray."

"Thank you, Mr. Traux," she says, sitting.

"How are you guys? Your mother has been texting me all morning about you guys coming up."

I smile. "We are good so far. I'll leave a bad review if I need to."

My father chuckles. "I'll check in later. No bad reviews from either of you."

Esmeray smiles, nodding as my father strolls away. "He's nice."

I sit. "When he wants to be."

"Least you don't have a father like Redmen."

Snorting, I agree. "Fuck, you're right."

She smiles, sipping her drink. "How have you been since…"

I almost died. "I think, good. No side effects. Went to a few appointments and no sign of the infection coming back."

She lets out a breath. "Good. Same here."

Rejected Wolf

I hate thinking about the day that she basically almost died. She had just walked out of the woods and then collapsed in my arms. My shoulder was torn to shreds from a demon wolf, but I stayed awake to see her. I didn't want to leave her side in case she died, but as soon as we got to the shifter hospital, I passed out.

Sailor sets down the charcuterie board—something I'd normally not order, but I think Esmeray will like it. And I was right, her eyes lit up at the various meats, cheese, crackers and fruit covering the board. "Refill?" Sailor asks us, looking at me more.

"Baby?" I ask Esmeray with a shake of my head.

"I will. Why aren't you having more?"

"Driving, and we have lots more to do."

She reaches around the board, touching my hand. "You're such a good boyfriend."

I bite back my smirk.

"Oh, how long have you guys been dating?" Sailor questions.

Esmeray sends me a worried look. I can tell she doesn't lie often.

"For a few months, but we are mates so, you know how it is." I offer up.

My girl's eyes soften, and she looks down.

Sailor snorts. "No one thought Krew would ever get a mate. It's even crazier saying it in the same sentence."

I keep my eyes on my girl. "Yeah, me neither, but I met Esmeray and things changed." She meets my eyes and I wink at her. "What would you like to try first on the board, babe?"

Sailor finally lets us be, and hopefully stops trying to flirt with me.

"Uh, surprise me?

Rejected Wolf

Esmeray

Krew opens the door for me, letting me step into his car. The whole date, we've been talking and laughing. He talks to me like we aren't mates and are just normal people on a date. He rounds the car, saying goodbye to his dad before hopping in and speeding off.

"I had fun, Krew. Thank you. The food was amazing!" I break the silence in the car.

He shakes his head, smiling. "Oh, we are not done. We have a few more hours together."

I smile. "Oh? What's next?"

He returns the smile with a boyish grin. I can tell he doesn't want to fully tell me yet, but he breaks,

"Do you want to get your nails done first or shop first?"

I think for a second. "Uh. Let's... shop first but won't you be wasting a lot of money?" Although the check was paid for by his dad, Krew left a tip. I can only imagine how much all of that was.

"It's not a waste. I actually earned this money to spend on you."

My heart swells as I brush my hair out of my face. "Well, I don't want you to use it on me!"

His ring finger touched my thigh before it settles there. "Hush, baby. I want to do this for you. Plus, you need new pants and thongs."

I suck my teeth. "How do you know?"

Krew chuckles. "I asked Stone where they all went..."

My cheeks heat up as I think of all the times Stone ripped the panties off me. He was making a habit of doing it and not rebuying them for me. "Well still, you don't have to do that for me."

Krew pulls into a parking spot in the shopping center nearby. He leans over the middle part, whispering, "I want something to rip off of you too."

I look at him, heat rolling in my lower stomach. "Krew..."

His eyes drop to my lips, and he doesn't hesitant to take my lips into his. I reach up, touching his smooth, sharp jaw. It's a brief sweet kiss though as he pulls back prematurely. "Come on. Let's go."

I rub his jaw. "Home? To have sex?"

He chuckles. "Now look who wants me really badly."

"You had your orgasm. I didn't," I tease.

"I'd fuck you right here if it didn't risk someone seeing your fine ass. So, for now, let's go shopping."

I let out a huff. "Fine... I guess. But I don't want much!"

But of course, we spent an hour picking out matching shoes and clothes. I can't pass up matching with him at any point. *I didn't want to hurt his feelings, of course.*

The nail place is nearby, and we browse as I let him pick out the colors of my nails.

"I like the white," Krew confirms.

"Will you match with me?" I tease.

He freezes, glancing at me. "Yeah, if you want me to."

I giggle. "I was kidding!"

Krew shakes his head. "Too late. I've already decided. White it is."

I figured he'd just get a mani, but no, he went all out and we got matching mani and pedis. I can't help but gush over him doing this with me. We talk the whole time, about nothing and everything. It was nice and relaxing and before I knew it, I was home, and our morning date was over.

Rune Hunt

I walk in, giggling at Krew about his joke. I look around the house, feeling a pull to the living room. *My guys are there.* I click my way over with Krew behind me.

Kai sits up, looking like he just woke up. *Were they bored?* "Hey, did you have fun?"

Zeno glance up from his handheld games. Stone is sprawled out across the couch, snoring away.

"Yeah! I did." I touch Kai's shoulders, dropping my bags near him and kicking off my heels, finally. My feet feels all sorts of relief once they are off.

Krew follows as I sit next to the sleeping Stone. "What did you guys do?"

Kai shrugs. "Watched movies and played video games."

I smile. "Sounds fun."

Kai grabs my hand, looking at the pure white acrylics. "Looks good. I like it when you have nails, you give the best back scratches."

"Look at Krew's."

Krew doesn't hide it, showing off his white nails.

"Pussy whipped." Zeno snorts, turning back to his games. "And he hasn't even had the pussy yet."

Krew growls. "Neither have you, ass."

I pout, crawling over to Zeno. "So, you wouldn't get your nails done with me?"

167

Rejected Wolf

He glances up, seeing my big doe eyes and stuck out lip. "I never said that, Mami."

I snort. "You all are whipped! Admit it." I throw myself onto Zeno, propping my legs up on Stone's chest. He stirs but doesn't wake up. I wonder how many times I've kept him up late with my bullshit.

"I will gladly admit it," Krew says, shredding his shirt, with only a tank top underneath. I hope my night ends with some of that. "But you love us."

I've never told them I loved them, so his comment makes me freeze. I thought it'd be too soon to say that. "I guess..." I tease, leaning back and covering Zeno's game with my hand. "What are you playing?"

"Nothing now. I can't see," he says with a smile, bending down to kiss my lips softly. "I'm glad you had fun with Krew, now you get to have fun with me tonight."

My brows pull together. "Huh?"

"We are going out tonight," he clarifies.

"Another date?"

He nods.

"With you?"

He nods again.

I look back at Krew, wondering if that was okay. We had an amazing time: wouldn't it be disrespectful? But he smiles at me. "You are going to have fun with him, baby."

Rune Hunt

Joy fills my chest, and I smile hard. "When do we leave?"

Zeno pats my head. "In a few hours."

I bite my lip. "What do I wear?! Two dates in one day. Why? What did you guys *do*? Is someone in trouble?"

Krew throws his head back with a laugh. "Nothing. We just figured you would like to get out of the house. You've been stuck inside."

I bit my lip. "Yeah... But you guys don't need to do that. I'm just glad you guys came."

"Yeah. Yeah. Humble shit, Esmeray," Krew says, throwing himself over the back of the couch. "But do you ever realize," he looks at me, "that we want to do this for you?"

I make a face. "Why?"

Zeno touches the tip of my nose cutely. "Because we care about you."

"Or," I rebuttal. "You guys pity my shortcomings."

Kai snorts. "You think we take your past 'shortcomings'?"

I nod, toeing Stone's neck. He turns over, grabbing my toes and rubbing them lightly.

Krew rolls his hazel eyes, brows pulling together. "That's my job..." He pouts.

I spread my legs, holding up my other foot. "I have two."

Rejected Wolf

He grabs it and rubs it. "Don't you guys like the white?"

Zeno nods, focusing on his game that he has now resting on my face. "Mhm."

Kai snorts. "Surprised you don't have matching toes."

I glance over at Krew, biting back a giggle. He smirks, looking down at my toes.

"Yeah! What kind of pussy whipped boy would do that? *Me? Never!*" Krew says sarcastically.

Kai's hazel eyes widen. "No fucking way! Liar!"

Once again, I had a guy pick out what I wore and he was a hundred percent accurate, although I'm still unsure where we are going. Zeno picked out a black shimmer dress that I can't wear underwear with because it has slit openings crawling up the side of the dress, until it gets the corset crop top with thin spaghetti straps holding them up. This dress fits like a pencil skirt, hugging my wide hips and thighs, with the top pushing out my breasts, perfectly spilling a bit.

These men definitely know what they like. My hair is down in wavy curls that hid the white patches on my back. I know they are there. Zeno knows they are there. My makeup—*thanks for buying, Krew*—is matching the dark look of my dress.

I grab my purse again, sliding my phone in. I've never been a purse kind of girl with good reason. People could easily steal it from me.

I don't know where we are going, so I can't judge what to bring and what not to bring.

My heels tap as I make my way out of the room to the steps and carefully go down. The heels he picked out are skinnier than what Krew had picked out before. *If I'm not careful, I'll bust my ass.*

Krew peeks out from the living room. "Goddamn."

My face heats up as I finally make it to him. He has a boyish grin on his pink lips. Holding out his hand, he guides me to the living room where Stone is up by now, eyes glued to my body. Zeno stands, basically drooling.

But I'm drooling over him.

He's wearing a short sleeve button up that has a few buttons open to show off his necklace and bits of chest hair. He has on khaki pants with boots. His hand with ringed fingers and a bracelet runs through his thick black hair that is down.

"Goddamn…" Kai says, eyes widening.

I glance down at myself, wondering if all this cleavage showing would piss them off, not to mention the slit sides. "Is it too revealing?"

"No," Zeno says, moving to me. "You look so stunning." His fingers run down my back, filling me with heat. I am on edge. I haven't been satisfied by Krew or anyone, and that's all I want.

Fuck the dates. I just want to be fucked... Just kidding. I love the dates.

"Fucking stunning. I'm jealous," Stone says, fixing his crotch on his shorts. "Fuckers..."

I snort. "Please, you get me twenty-four seven. We fuck every night."

Kai nods. "I'm more jealous that Zeno gets to look at that all night."

Stone nods in agreement.

"Where are we going?" I ask, leaning into Zeno for support. I'm going to get Krew to rub my feet tonight. He'll probably do it without me asking for him to do it.

"Did Krew tell you where you were going?" he asks.

I huff. "No."

"Then I won't. It's a surprise." The last part he whispers deeply in my ear.

"I hate surprises," I groan.

"You liked mine today," Krew says. He has since changed into shorts from our date clothing. "Maybe you hate that you have to go on a date with Zeno."

I shake my head at his teasing. "At least he's cute to look at and listen to."

Krew scoffs at my diss. "Rude. My mother calls me cute so... Does your mother, Zeno?"

172

"I don't need her to." He shrugs.

I giggle at Krew's hurt face. "Come give me a kiss before I leave."

Kai is the closest, so he gets a kiss first. His hands stay on my hips, careful not to do anything more to me.

Krew runs his hands all over my body, pulling my dress a bit higher up my thighs. Pulling back, I hit his chest. "Hey!"

"Sorry." He gives me a goofy smile. "You look amazing."

I kiss his cheek lightly. "Thanks."

Stone is last, and definitely not shy about grabbing my ass and pulling me into his hard bulge. I grab his hips, giggling and leaning backwards to reach his lips. "Have fun, baby," he mutters into my lips.

I push him back. "I need better lipstick around you guys."

He smiles, deep red on his lips. "We can ruin it more if you want?"

That's all I want. I bite my lip lightly. *Wouldn't it be amazing to have all of them at once? Maybe I should cancel this date…*

But instead, I hook my arm around Zeno. "Let's leave before we never do. Bye, guys!"

They all call out after us. Like a true gentleman, Zeno opens the door of Kai's slick black Range Rover and closes it before hopping around to his seat.

Rejected Wolf

"So, where are we going?" I ask again when he starts driving.

He sends me a look. "Are you gonna be annoying the whole time?"

I giggle. "To you, yes."

Esmeray

The pull with Zeno is a strong desire and every day we tend to have a phone call to get each other off. It's becoming ridiculous how tight the need is inside of me. His hand on my thigh as he drives makes me want to go feral.

Zeno and I have gotten close, and he even told me about his shitty family and his overbearing, abusive parents. As Alpha, my rage comes out. As a mate, I want to protect him, like he actually needs it. We talked about my father a lot too. It's bittersweet because I just know my father would have loved them.

Rejected Wolf

Zeno has been so kind and loves to talk to me for hours sometimes. And as a mate, I want to bond with him more and more as we talk.

I spread my legs a bit, letting my dress ride up.

He glances over, eyes down at my thighs. His hand traces my inner thigh, teasing me. Heat runs through me as I swallow. "Do you realize…" His hand slips in between my legs, hand brushing my pussy. It's so light, it feels like warm air. I'm panting now, wanting him to soothe the aching inside of me. "How much I want you?" He chuckles. "Sadly, this place is like five minutes away because we don't have time."

I roll my eyes, turning and pulling myself to him. It makes his hand move closer to my pussy.

"Jesus." He groans. "Are you not wearing any panties?"

"With this dress?" I shake my head. "No."

His chest is heaving as his fingers run up my pussy until his thumb finds my clit. His rings make me shiver at the coldness touching my inner thighs. Then his thumb swirls my clit, making me moan softly. "I have to deal with this dancing all over me, all night?!"

My eyes open and I look up at him through my eyelashes. "What do you mean dancing?"

He smiles, rubbing my clit faster. My legs vibrate from the intense pleasure.

"Oh, fuck!" I throw my head back into the seat.

But then his thumb slides into my wet folds before slowly going inside of me. But he pulls out too quickly and *pops* the wet finger into his mouth. "Mhm," he hums, deeply. "I'm tasting you tonight."

I clench my legs together as my pussy pulses. "Taste me now."

He licks his lips. "Esmeray."

I glance down at his hard bulge through his dress slacks. I'm half tempted to pull it out and wrap my lips around him. "Zeno."

He glances at me, pulling into a parking lot. Once he shuts off the car, I hear the loud blaring of music coming from a club with bright neon lights. It looks just as fancy as the country club.

"Is this your dad's club?" I pry my eyes from the lights to look at him. He told me about this place before.

He shrugs. "Figured you might like it. You love music so…"

Sex… or dancing… How the fuck do I choose this? Fuck him while dancing? No… I let out a sigh. "Sex will have to wait again."

He smirks, pulling my chin so he can kiss my lips. "Be patient. It'll be worth it."

"I'm not patient at all. You know this." He knows because I beg for him to come fuck me each time his voice or videos give me an orgasm. And it is often.

He chuckles. "Come on, baby." He rounds the car before I can even hide my purse in his car because I didn't want to carry it. I did a quick text to the group

chat we have and let them know beforehand. I step out
of the car, taking his open hand.

Zeno's hand stays on mine the whole time as he
leads me to the front of the building. He doesn't lead
me to the long line of people waiting to get in, instead
we go straight to the bouncer. I almost feel bad for
those that have been waiting.

Inside, the dance music blares, vibrating on the
floor. People dance close to one another on the bright,
glowing dance floor. Most of them look like they are
fucking. So maybe, just maybe, I can get away with
fucking Zeno right here, but he'd never let me do that.
Not in his dad's club.

I see Zeno's lips move lightly, making me
glance over. "What?"

He pulls me into him when we got to the bar.
His lips press against my ear and when I feel his breath
against my skin, I shudder. "Listen to me and only
me."

I blink a few times before I realize he wants me
to use my little wolf ears to be able to hear him. With a
deep breath, I hone in on the wolf inside of me, doing
everything I was taught. The music fades to a dull roar
and the chatter around us is gone.

"Can you hear me?" he asks. It sounded so
clear like it was only me and him in the room.

I look up, laughing. "I did it!"

His hands find my waist as he turns to the
bartender and orders a drink for us.

"You're definitely not twenty-one." I mutter.

The bartender is quick, and Zeno is quick to leave a big tip and pay him. "Perks of having a rich daddy."

"I have four," I mutter.

His eyes glance at me, chuckling. "Want to dance?"

I down the alcohol, nodding. Warmth swirls as it hits my stomach. "Please?"

His fuzzy jaw drops. "You know that's straight vodka?"

I blink up at him. "Do you want to dance with me or not?"

He smirks, downing his drink and nodding. I grab his hand, just as he puts down the glass, and pull him out to the dance floor. My hips are already shaking to the pop music and I'm sure he's looking at my ass, because when I glance back, his eyes glance back up.

Once I get to a place that is comfortable, he pulls me close. His hand runs up my back a bit before we begin to dance together. Our hips and movement are sync to the point where I think he and I practiced this.

Is this what High School Musical *feels like?*

My hand travels up his chest, feeling all the muscled ridges. It stops on his chest as his hands run down over my hips. His hands are warm with each movement, making my body ache for him.

179

Rejected Wolf

Our eyes lock. His face is a bit hard to see under this lighting, but I can tell his dark eyes are clouded with lust.

I smirk. *You wanted to wait.*

So, for the next half an hour, I danced against his boner while he whispered sweet words in my ear. We dance in rhythm, and grind on each other.

The pressure of an orgasm builds in my hips, aching to be released. My plan backfires, because when I dance on his thick thigh, the pressure builds and I almost moan.

I pull back, chest heaving. My clit has rubbed against his thigh one too many time, urging an orgasm closer and closer. "I, uh, I have to pee." I push past him, finding the restroom without help. My body aches for a release I knew he won't give me. Not yet anyways.

The door swings behind me close before it swings open. I jolt, not expecting anyone to follow me. Before I can process anything, Zeno cups my cheeks, pulling my lips harshly into his.

My eyes widen before heat sets in deep in my hips. I grab at his waist and kiss him back, hard. Our touch is feverish, trying to get close to each other. He steps forward, knocking my lower back into the counter. When I gasp, he slips his tongue into my mouth. He tastes of alcohol and sweat. His hands drop and grip my thighs, lifting me onto the counter.

Everything is happening so fast, but I didn't want him to slow down. I pull away, gasping as I reach for his belt. He helps, frantically to get it off as he moves between my legs.

"Fuck," he mutters, finally freeing his veiny cock.

Fuck yes, finally.

The door swings open, making us jolt and him put his beautiful dick away. A drunk girl stumbles inside, groaning as she moves into the stall and closes it behind her.

Zeno meets my eyes, smirking.

I break out into a giggle, before opening my legs again.

"Let's go home, Esmeray," he whispers. "There... I'll fuck you."

A whine crawls from my throat. I was tired of waiting.

He chuckles, pulling me from the counter and fixing my dress to come down on my thighs. "Come on." He leads the way out of the bathroom, through the dance floor and to the car. Each step is torture with wetness soaking my thighs as my hips ache horribly.

Is this "blue balls" for women?

He helps me into the car, fingers brushing my inner thighs. I send him a look and he sends me a knowing smirk.

Zeno rounds the car and I watch him climb in the car. His boner is poking through his pants and as his ringed fingers wrap around the steering wheel, something whines inside of me.

Mate. a faint voice says inside of me.

My eyes brows pull together. *What was that?*

He takes off, driving towards the house. His hand rests on my thighs, making me squirm.

"I haven't had an orgasm all day," I mutter. "Just cockblocking after cockblocking."

He chuckles. "So, how bad is it?" His hand runs under my skirt, close to my core, and just that makes me quiver and moan. "Fuck." He says almost breathlessly. He's not even touching my pussy, but can he feel how hot or wet I am?

"No one wants to make me come! Everyone wants to see me suffer!" I whine.

His thumb swirls around my clit once he finds it, making me cry out a bit. I am so close to orgasming. The buildup was from the morning with the twins, then Krew, and now this. He smirks and says huskily, "You want me to stop?"

I grab his wrist, just to hold him closer and to not let him pull away. "Please, don't."

He swirls his thumb again, making me spread my legs. "You want me to make you come, baby?"

I nod.

"Beg for it or I stop."

I glance at him. *How serious is he about that?* But when he started pulling away, a whine creeps from

182

my throat. "Please, make me come, Zeno. I need it! Please, don't stop."

He listens, adding pressure into my clit, making me moan out. I drop my head back, swirling my hip with his movement. It brought me so close to the edge.

"Fuck!" I dig my nails into his skin as the pressure tightens. "Please, don't stop. I'm so fucking close." I gasp, legs shaking and body tingling. White dances behind my eyelids and my body stiffens and arches. "Fuck. Fuck. Please, Zeno. Please!"

But he fucking pulls away.

I cry out in frustration as the orgasm fades. "No! Zeno. Please. I'm begging you, make me come. Please!"

But he uses two hands to pull over to the side of the road in a clearing. He slams on the brakes, putting it in park before shifting and coming back to me.

I twist to him, letting him shove his pointer and ring finger inside of my soaking pussy. Those are the only two fingers without rings. I cry out as they sink inside, and his thumb finds my clit again.

I look at him. "Please, don't stop."

He licks his lips. "You want it that bad?"

I nod, closing my eyes. His two fingers curl upward, playing with my wall. That and the pressure on my clit sends me to the edge very quickly. I throw my head back, crying out. "Please, don't stop! Please don't fucking stop. I-I'm coming! I'm coming!" I arch my back, feeling euphoria crash straight into me. I cry and whine as I come undone right around his fingers. When I come back down from cloud nine, I lick my lips, shuddering.

Zeno pulls back and I hear his belt buckle rattle. "Come ride me."

I open my eyes, looking at him. He had pushed his chair back and is now pulling down his pants and freeing his cock.

"I need you. Come here," he mutters.

I crawl carefully over the middle and straddle his thighs. His hand jerks up and down his thick dick as his eyes stay on my face. The free hand pushes my dress up past my hips. "How badly do you want me?"

He grunts. "Stop it and ride me."

My brow cocks. "Should I?

He grasps my neck, pulling me close to his face. "Just because you're my alpha, doesn't mean I won't fuck your pussy hard, Esmeray. Don't play with what's mine."

My lips drop open. "Take what's yours then, Papi."

We share a harsh kiss as he positions and shoves himself inside of me. We moan out together. His cock stretches me and twitches with a pulse.

After a split second, we began fucking each other like we've never fucked anyone before. I use my knees to bounce on him, hands against the roof to protect my head from hitting it. My moans echo. *I don't even care how loud I am right now.*

His hips thrusts upward, slamming into me every time I lower myself. His hands reach up, pulling my top down, so my bouncing breasts are exposed. Instantly, his hot mouth captures my nipple.

I arch, pleasure rushing through me straight to my dripping core. "Fuck!" I reach down and begin unbuttoning his shirt which was so hard to do while bouncing. With his help, he shreds his shirt, pressing his warm chest into mine as he kisses my lips.

"You feel so fucking good, baby," he says with a moan and leans back. "Ride me, baby." He lets me bounce on him as he sits back, watching me. I bit my lip, doing the best I can. "Good fucking girl. Take my dick." He grasps my neck, head dropping back as he moans. "Keep going."

"Maybe I'll stop like you've been doing," I say breathlessly. But with the pressure building, I had no intentions of stopping but he didn't know that.

"Not a fucking option," he growls, grasping my neck hard and pounding up into me.

My mouth drops open as waves of pleasure follows each stroke. He's hitting such a sweet spot.

His cock twitches inside of me. "Esmeray." He moans, closing his eyes.

One of my hands grabs his shoulder, the other digs my nails in his abs. His abs tighten as our loud

185

moans muddle together.

"I'm coming, Zeno!" I throw my head back.

His thrusts become erratic, and he barely lets me move. He slams into me over and over, making me cry out until finally I cry his name and come undone.

He slams into me as he finally comes with a low groan. His cock twitches hard, emptying inside of me.

I can't move. I can't think. I can barely remember where I am or even remember how to breath. My body tingles with a release, I've been wanting all day. I blink away cloud nine, feeling my body relax. *Holy fuck...* I close my eyes, trying to calm my beating chest. My body is slick with sweat and it's hot in the car.

"Fuck." I hear him breath out harshly.

I lean forward, burying my face into his neck. "Bad *fuck*? Or good *fuck*?"

He chuckles. "Good, idiot." His hand rubs my back a bit, pulling my damp hair to the side.

After a few quiet moments, I sit up, "Zeno..."

He looks up, blinking.

I wiggle my hips a bit. "You're still inside of me and hard..."

"Who said we are done?"

I smirk. *No one did.*

Esmeray

"How was your date?" Krew asks, eating chips on the couch. Kai has fallen asleep on the couch and Stone is engrossed in a book.

I throw myself down next to him, smirking. "Not as great as yours, Krew."

Krew smirks. "Told you she liked me better."

Zeno throws his hair up as he chuckles. "Sure, Krew, you win."

My face heat up as I think about how many times, we had sex in his car. Twice in the front and again in the back before we finally decide to come back. "You guys leave tomorrow?" I question, leaning onto Stone. His hand rubs my back.

"Mhm," Krew says, almost sounding as sad as I am.

I bit my lip. "Slumber party?"

Stone raises a brow. "What?"

"Like… Like, you move the beds to the floor, and we all cuddle together and make me less sad about you guys going."

"Oh!" Krew snorts. "I call small spoon with Zeno!"

I giggle, looking at Zeno who rolls his eyes. Krew and Zeno seem to be like good friends, especially with Zeno helping him with work. Kai and Stone seem like good friends too, and I know Kai would have been his beta. "Let me shower. Stone, you are in charge of the slumber party for now."

He smirks. "Oh, thanks. We all have good experiences with this."

Giggling, I kiss his cheek before moving out of the living room. Zeno's hand spanks my ass as I move from the room. I giggle again, running up the stairs to get cleaned up.

We spend hours talking while lying on the floor. A movie plays in the background that we aren't listening to. I giggle with them as we all bond and they get to know me better. I don't even want to sleep. I don't want to sleep because I know they will be gone tomorrow by noon. Just the thought of it makes my chest ache. I don't want to be without them. The distance hurts more than Reed not talking to me. Talking to them and texting them sucked.

That's why shifting is so important to me. I want to be living with them again. I doubt any of them want to be back living with their parents. The freedom to do what we want and when we want was bliss.

I snap a group photo and send it to Reed.

Me: Missing out.

I hate how hung up on Reed I am. I never got close to him and yet, I feel the thread between us. There's a pull there. Mates are important. Most wolves get only one. The bond between two mates is unbreakable. I think about my dream… *Was it really a dream? Did Reed reject our bond before it could even form?*

Stone and I have the strongest bond, only because we spend most of our time together.

Kai seems to be like a beta to me. He's a perfect mentor, and never gets mad when I become frustrated or mess up.

Krew is the goofy one, making me laugh whenever I start feeling bad. We share looks and end up laughing harder than before.

Zeno is calm and keeps me that way even though we both just went feral, fucking each other.

They all treat me like I'm a goddess to them, and never let me feel not beautiful. They are everything to me.

Rejected Wolf

I wake up between Zeno and Krew which makes me warm. Zeno is awake, whispering to Stone about some new workout and guy shit. I roll over, touching Zeno's chest. He glances over with a small, tired smile.

I give him a quick kiss before kissing Stone and going to the bathroom with my phone. I don't even bother closing the door. At this point, they've all seen me in one way or another.

Well not Krew...

I open my phone, sitting on the toilet, almost pissing myself when I see Reed has sent me a message. This whole month, he's been ignoring me. I hope he's thought about us and wants to apologize.

But my heart drops.

It's a picture of him with some blonde-haired girl and their lips are connected. They both have smiles on their lips. It's sent with a text that says, "He's not even thinking about you, whore. He rejected you."

I swallow hard, setting my phone down. Tears sting in my eyes as I stare at the wall. *Don't you dare cry in front of your mates.* I wipe away my tears before finishing up and moving back out. *So, it was true. Reed rejected me at the academy... when I was dying...*

Stone looks up at me. "Are you okay?"

"Mhm." I fake a smile before crawling in between him and Zeno. Warmth fills me as they move closer to me. I bury my face against Zeno's chest as Stone wraps his arm around my waist.

190

"Are you sure you're okay?" Zeno says.

I just nod.

That picture confirmed the rejection wasn't a dream. He rejected me... He doesn't want our bond. He doesn't want this pack. He doesn't care.

"Are you sad we are leaving?" he mutters.

I let out a huff. "Don't remind me. Continue on with your conversation. I'll be here." I sink lower, wrapping my arm around his waist. I barely listen to them as they speak about nothing really. I try to ease my chest pain. It feels like my heart was broken. Why, though? He barely bonded with me. It shouldn't hurt this much.

I keep seeing the girl with him behind my eyelids. His arms around her and their lips connected. *Does he love her? Is that his mate? Do I mean nothing? Of course, I mean nothing. He ignores me, called me names, and even turned my mates against me. I was the alpha female who came along and ruined everything. I ruined things for him. I took his title. I took his friends.*

Zeno rubs the back of my neck, running up into my hair. He reminds me that he's here for me. His chest vibrates with each word he says, humming into mine.

He's gonna leave me and I'm not sure when the next time I'll see him.

"Do I get cuddles?" Krew says, stretching.

191

Zeno jerks his chin to him. I crawl over Zeno, moving to Krew. He scoops me into his arms.

"I meant Z, but this will do," he jokes. It makes me smile a bit. I straddle his hips, pressing my cheek into his chest. *My goofball.*

He would be gone soon too.

His arms wrap around me, one climbing up my back to my hair. "I'm gonna miss you, E."

Inhaling his scent, I clench my jaw. "Thanks... for the date."

Krew presses his chin against my head. "Plenty more where that came from."

I smirk. The bed shifts as Kai sits up and runs a hand through his hair. He's shirtless and that doesn't even warm me up.

Reed hurt me. Now my mates are leaving.

Life is so unpredictable. I didn't know I'd wake up and one day be an alpha. I didn't know that Reed would *actually* move on so quickly. I didn't know if the four guys around me were going to do the same because they don't love me anymore.

It's hard to know what's going to happen next sometimes.

Zeno lives farther away than the twins do. But who knows when the twins' parents will let them out of their clutches? Krew explains that he liked to work at least three days a week at night at Zeno's brother's shop. But he wants to do more.

Would my father be like this if he were alive?

Rune Hunt

Kai's alarm goes off which he twists and turns off.

Krew rolls, grounding himself into my core. I gasp, a faint heat rushing through me. "We have thirty minutes to have sex." He says in a raspy voice.

I smirk. "Good for you, we only need five."

He scoffs, sitting up. "I'll have you know; I'll last at least seven minutes this time."

It actually makes me roll my eyes with a real smile. *That's what I mean. He makes me smile when I don't want to.*

Sadness fills me right after. *He's going to be gone for a while. Who am I to be selfish? He has a life. His life doesn't revolve around me.*

I run my hands up his abs and chest and pull him back down. I kiss his lips briefly, and he looks down at me with soft hazel eyes. *Can he feel my sadness? I know the others might and not know why I'm truly sad, but can he?*

"What?" I question.

"Are you okay?"

I scoff. "Why does everyone keep asking that?"

He shrugs. "Just wanted to fucking know if you'd miss me."

I push at him, trying to get away. "Not at all."

He chuckles, grabbing my hips. "Yeah? Please! You love me more than any of them."

193

Rejected Wolf

"Asshole." Zeno scoops me away from him, making me giggle. "She hates you the most."

Krew tackles us both on the bed. "Take that back! Tell him you love me the most." His fingers tickle my side, and I can't help but laugh and try to thrash away from him.

After they leave, my mood tanks, and I barely get out of bed. Stone tries to get me to eat but being away from them and often staring at the photo with Reed and the girl, my chest aches so badly. My head pounds against my skull each time I get up to even take a piss.

Stone has been helpful but concerned.

I don't bother telling him what's wrong, instead I endure this alone. This happened for days and each day he comforts me the best he can and even calls the guys for us all to just talk for a few hours.

It's nice, although it's making me feel guilty. I'm sure they'd rather be with me too, and they feel something.

By Wednesday, I finally pull myself out of bed, even though my head is spinning. I move to the steaming shower of Stone's room. I open the shower door. The steam hits my face and Stone barely turns, probably hearing me or sensing me.

"Can I join?" I ask.

Stone looks up, wet droplets run down his body and soap covers some of his body. He smiles, nodding.

Rune Hunt

I undress, right in front of his watchful eyes, stepping inside.

"How are you feeling?" he mutters, slowly and hesitantly pulling me flush against him.

"Headache, dizzy." Not to mention the horrible chest pains that feel like I might have a heart attack soon. I press my breasts into his soapy sternum, running my hands over his hips.

"Do you want to talk about why you've been in a depressive mood since Sunday?" Stone questions, running his hands over my wet skin.

"Do I have to?"

He shrugs.

"I don't feel like talking. Thought we could do a little of not talking before we work out today."

"If you're not in the mood, Esmeray... Don't push yourself," he says, running a hand over my soaking wet hair.

I tilt back to look up at him. "It's important to me that we at least work on me shifting."

He nods. "But I find I can't shift when I have a lot on my mind."

"Kai told you that? Because he said the same to me."

"And it's true, Esme."

I roll my eyes, pulling his lips down to mine. "Just make me forget everything for five minutes." I fist his hard cock.

Rejected Wolf

He smiles. "Unlike Krew," he moves his lips from my lips, down to my jaw, "I will last long."

I snort. "Oh really? I doubt that."

His lips move up to my earlobe, sucking on it. "Let me show you."

Stone

I fuck Esmeray slow and soft against the shower wall, bringing her to a quick orgasm that makes her cry my name over and over until I feel her juices running down my cock. It brings me to an orgasm quickly after as her walls clench around me.

She lays her head against my shoulder, chest pounding heavily against mine.

"Did it worsen your headache?"

She shakes her head. "No, it helped a bit. Maybe if you fuck me ten more times, my headaches will be fully gone."

I chuckle.

"Let's try."

Ignoring her, I clean her up, and carry her out into the bedroom. "You should rest."

"After we work out and after breakfast," she says.

I didn't want her to workout. But would she be too stubborn to listen to me? Of course. Alpha does what alpha wants.

So, we work out, and it seems to help take stress off her. She moves lighter during our workout, focusing on the playlist we made together. I watch her.

Esmeray has come a long way and is so much different than what she was before she knew she was an alpha. She's strong, even though I can tell she's sadder than before. I think it's the distance from everyone, especially Reed.

He's not texting us or her.

Give him time, I keep telling myself. *But how much time does the kid need to finally come around?* I know he's pissed he has to listen to a female. I know he's pissed his mate has five mates, but the way he's been treating Esmeray is unacceptable.

Part of me doesn't want her to accept him. She chooses it, and I will respect whatever she chooses after I kick his ass.

Krew told me everything that Reed has said about her, and I hate it. I understand why Krew punched Reed.

"What's wrong?" Esmeray asks, wiping sweat from her forehead.

I shrug. "Thinking."

"Do you want to go for a run?"

"Are you sure you're up for it, E?" She nods. I didn't want to push her, but I know she won't listen. Alphas are so stubborn. I shred my tank top, feeling her eyes on me. Our eyes meet and I drop my shorts and boxers.

Esmeray smiles, making my cock twitch. I'm always hard around her, whenever she touches me or even speaks to me. I feel like a teenage boy again, getting hard over the sight of a round ass. Her golden-brown eyes flicker to my cock.

I raise a brow. "You like, baby?"

She chuckles. "Yes, daddy. I do like."

But before she can touch me, I inhale, calling on my wolf. My bones crack and stretch into my wolf form. Fur crawls across my body, making me shudder and shake out the fur.

Like routine, she reaches and touches my fur. Her touch soothes my hot skin. Shifting is hard sometimes. Sometimes it hurts. Sometimes it feels like my skin is going to boil off.

"Wolves are so beautiful," she declares.

No. I'm beautiful. I shake my fur once more before moving to the back door. She opens it for me, and I step out, paws digging into the dirt. Inhaling, I smell the squirrel's eating acorns, the fresh grass and even her.

I look back at Esmeray. She fixes her loose ponytail as I inhale her more. She smells earthy and calm like a morning fresh dew.

"Ready?"

I look up at her, nodding. As soon as I turn back around, I take off, racing to the tree line.

Esmeray takes off: her footsteps stomping after me. She's usually lighter than this, but that's okay. I don't run as fast as I can. She's tired, I know she is.

Our routine takes longer than normal from having to stop a lot. She holds her chest each time trying to catch her breath. After the third time, I feel like something is off.

She leans against a tree. "One second..."

I shift back, pushing my wolf away. Just as I get to my feet, Esmeray's eyes roll back, and she begins going down. I rush forward, catching her body. "Esmeray. Esmeray!"

I pace the room. Claire has come over after Esmeray passed out. I called her mates, but not Reed, and now we just wait for Claire to come back out.

Kai grabs my shoulder. "Calm down, Stone, before you create a fucking hole in the floor."

I send him a glare. "How are you so calm?"

"Because she's going to be okay."

"How do you know that?" Krew asks.

Kai let out a breath. "Because she always is…"

"It could be the infection and—"

The front door opens, making us look up from the living room. Zeno scans the house before laying eyes on us. "Where is she?"

I let out a huff of air. "Upstairs. Claire won't let us up, only Silver and Kira."

Zeno looks up the stairs, weighing the options.

"Come sit, Zeno," Liza, my mother, offers.

Zeno lets out a sigh and moves to us. "What's going on?" He looks to me like I have the answer. *The thing is, I should have the answers. She was with me the whole time. I was supposed to be watching her. I should know exactly what's going on, but I don't.* I open my mouth, not knowing what to say. If I say what I want to say—*the truth*—and I was them, I'd knock me the fuck out.

But behind me, footsteps start down the steps. I twist to look up at Silver and Claire coming down the steps, Kira must still be with Esmeray.

"Is she awake?" I question, making the guys all stand. I feel their worry running down our bond and Zeno's rage, but hopefully, it's not at me.

Claire shakes her head, a silver dread falling against her face. "Not yet, at least. I just have a few questions. Sit, please."

I run a hand through my hair, listening and sitting. We all crowd the couch while Silver and Claire stand near the television.

"What's going on?" Zeno asks, leg bouncing.

Fuck. I feel so guilty.

"Is she pregnant?" my sister asks, earning a glare from me.

Logically, I know she's not. She just got put on birth control, but still, I wait for Claire's answer.

"No, sweetheart."

Ivory sits back. "Darn…"

I roll my eyes. I doubt we need *that* when demon wolves are attacking the academy and after Esmeray.

"How was Esmeray before she passed out?" Claire asks me.

"Sad, more so than usual," I answer, feeling more guilty I can't make her happy.

"We had just left this Sunday from a weekend stay," Kai informs. "We thought she just missed us."

Claire nods.

Kira appears from the doorway, and I stand, hoping she's going to tell me something I want to hear but she shakes her head. "She's not awake."

I groan, flopping back down.

"She's been complaining about chest pains and a headache to me a lot."

Zeno blinks. "To just you?"

She shrugs.

"I've never heard her complain more than a normal amount. What about you guys?" he asks us.

I shake my head. "Not a lot."

Claire touches her chin. "Effects from those demonic wolves?"

I twist to Krew. He looks at all the eyes staring him down. "I feel fine. Good even. Not many headaches or chest pains of any sort."

My mother stands. "Sil, do you know what this sounds like?"

"Hmm?"

"The same thing Vixen went through with Ricci."

I frown. "Aunt Vix?"

She nods but watches my father. His brows pull together before nodding, "Claire, do you know what I'm talking about?"

It takes Claire a second to catch on as well. "Yes, I think so."

"Good," Zeno says in an annoyed voice. "Someone explain it to us, please." I don't blame him. I didn't like to be left out of the telepathic conversation they were having. It's not like we know what Vixen went through. Vixen was my aunt with three mates. She wasn't the alpha. She was a packmate. The only one that wasn't her mate was the guy named Ricci. But they seem to both be okay with that.

"Ricci is the fourth mate of Vixen," my mother explains. "A long time ago, they were dating before any of the others, until she finally told them she has a pull with all of them. He broke things off, and eventually he moved on to being the alpha of his own pack. Vixen wasn't okay, even though she had three other mates and no matter what, she just felt this extreme pain in her chest like someone had broken her heart."

"What happened?" Kai questions.

My mother sighs. "Ricci had rejected her, and she refused to give him up until it almost killed her."

My eyes narrow as rage runs through my chest. "You think Reed rejected her, because I know damn well none of us did."

"It's just a possibility," my father says, trying to calm me down.

But I couldn't. If he did, why didn't she tell me or the others?

Zeno's jaw is tightening. "What..." He takes a deep breath. "What other symptoms of rejection are there?"

Kai looks down, but answers. "Chest pains, shortness of breath, headaches, uncontrollable shifting and unregulated feelings. It feels like... you are dying from a broken heart.

Claire nods. "It could be what's holding her back from shifting."

That was enough. I pull out my phone, instantly calling Reed. It rings one time, but then goes straight to voicemail. "Fucking bitch," I grumble and redial it. The same thing happens. I want to crush the phone in my hand. Moving from the living room to the foyer and continue to call. The eleventh time, Reed finally picks up.

"What the fuck do you—" he starts.

"What did you do?" It's all I can manage to get out before taking deep breaths.

"Huh?"

"What did you do to Esmeray?"

It's silent for a moment. "What's wrong with her? Is she okay?"

"Don't act like you fucking care!" I snap, anger rising quickly. "She's fucking dying and passing out and—"

"Dying?! Again."

I pull the phone away from my ear before taking a deep breath. "Reed…"

"Stone…" he deadpans.

"You rejected her, didn't you?"

It's silent.

"Yes, or no? Because she's trying to hold on to your dumb ass and it's weakening her and making her physically die."

It's silent again. "I'm on my way."

"No!"

He hangs up.

"Fuck!" My fist clenches the phone so tight I think it will snap in half. Rage is making me shake. He didn't seem to care that Esmeray was dying. *He never did.* When he gets to the house, I'm beating his ass.

"He hung up?" Kai asks me.

Rejected Wolf

"He didn't answer my question but he's on his way."

"Great... Is there a way that Esmeray will feel better?" Kai asks, turning back to Claire. I step closer to hear what they are going to say.

Claire nods, sitting on the large couch now. "Reed has to either take back his rejection or she cuts ties."

My jaw tightens. "She let the fucker get away with it for this long, I doubt she'll cut ties."

Krew leans back, sighing. "All because he rejected her. She's enduring all this pain. Does he know what it does to mates?"

Zeno hits his shoulder. "You barely did. I doubt that idiot knows."

I stand tall. "I am beating the shit out of him."

"Stone," my dad warns.

I hold up my hands. "I'm not the alpha, so I can *legally* beat the fuck out of him if I want."

My dad sends me a glare.

"Put yourself in my shoes," I mutter, turning to lean against the wall, and look up the stairs. *None of this is going to go well.*

Esmeray

Whispers fill the forest surrounding me, eerily.
Goosebumps rise against my skin. I glance around.
Where am I? Why am I here?

The air around me thickens with something
sinister. I twist and twist until I see two wolves running
my way. Behind them are demon wolves. Their skin is
completely gone around their faces, leaving just a
skull. Black smoke is left in their wake as if they are on
fire.

One of the twin wolf's limps, yet still pushes
through the pain of its wound. The other runs behind
him and every time those wolves get close, he snaps

207

and attacks protectively. He turns to run around the first, meeting my eyes.

Run, *his voice echoes in my head like a record. His velvety voice is soft, yet familiar.*

I look at the demon wolves behind him. Tame them, *a female voice echoes in my head. As soon as the twins pass, I let out an alpha growl involuntary. It's loud and rumbling deep in my chest. All the demon wolves come to a rolling stop, digging their toes into the dirty ground. Their ears flatten as they begin to whine.*

There's no reason for these demon wolves to listen to me. *But they do, like I was their alpha.*

I glance back seeing the second black wolf staring at me. Hide.

Help us. Help us, please, *his voice cries in my head.*

I shoot up in the bed, shuddering from the dream. I look up to Kira, who watches me from the edge of the bed of my room.

"Are you okay?" she asks, touching my leg.

"What are you doing here?" I let out a shaky breath.

"You passed out. Fainted while running with Stone."

I swallow. I remember that. *Fuck.* "Is he okay?"

Her brows pull together. "That's what you care about. You could have been hurt."

Help us. Oni is back.

I freeze, holding up a hand. "Do you hear that?" It's the same male voice from my dream. I doubt Kira can hear what I hear. I feel like I might be going insane.

"What?" Her brows pull together. "What are you talking about?"

I shake my head, touching my forehead. "Just a voice in my head…"

She tries to speak again but the voice overpowers hers.

Alpha, help us.

"Esme?" She reaches out for me.

I shake my head, trying to calm the voice in my head. "It's from my dreams. These wolves…"

Then it dawns on me. The first night I woke up and we saw those wolves on the way back from the hospital… The voice in my head belongs to them. The first one that said help was this one: the one in my head. *Are they* endangered? *Am I connected?* Why, though? *Are they pack members?* I take a deep breath, channeling hard on the wolf that needs me. When my eyes open again, I see faint threads. It's a pale egg white, leading me somewhere out the house.

Blistering pain erupts in my shoulder, making my head spin.

"Esmeray?" Kira stands, moving to me.

Rejected Wolf

No! Oni! Stop! The voice screams. Then I feel it, pain aching my ribs like someone is tearing me to shreds.

I shoot from the bed, feeling the same pull that I felt with the rest of my pack. One of my pack members is around here and needs me.

"Esmeray!" Kira shouts, but I'm already out of the bedroom and rushing down the stairs.

I get the front door open before I hear Zeno's voice. "Esmeray?!"

"Follow!" I shout, running out the door. The pull is strong, and the pain is worse. It leads me to the woods in the back of the house. I glance back, seeing my pack and Silver coming after me. *Good. They followed me.*

"Esmeray!" Stone shouts. "Slow down!"

But I don't. I keep going, dodging the trees. My bare feet sting against the ground as my body aches. I can do this. They need me. I push myself hard, feeling sweat cake my body from the hot air.

"Hey! What's going on?!" Krew shouts.

I don't know. I don't know what's going on or what I'm even getting into. The closer I get, the stronger the thread and pull is. The pain also grows, almost slowing me down.

Then I see it. A demon wolf about to rip one of the white wolf's' throat out.

My pack. Pack. A voice in my head exclaims, guiding me faster than I've ever been.

210

Rune Hunt

Shift? I ask myself. *Do it. Save them. Save your pack.*

I jump through the air, but of course, I don't shift. Instead, I tackle the demon wolf and pull him from the wolf.

Krew curses before the sound of bones cracking fills the air. I feel each one of my packmates shift, although I can't see them.

I hold the wolf down with my foot. "Don't get bitten or scratched!" I order them as Stone's harsh growl sends one backwards.

The demon wolf below me snaps, earning a harsh deep growl from me. It cowards like the rest of the group does. I snap at it, daring it to do the same for me. Instead, it whines and escapes from my grasp, keeping its distance. *Why were they listening to me?*

Standing, I look at the white wolf that called to me.

Help.

I glance at my mates to make sure they are okay. They seem to be making a protective circle around me. Silver's wolf is enormous and a beautiful, snow white like his son's. I follow the wolf to a tree where the black wolf is. Blood leaks from the wounds, matting his dark fur "Fuck." I reach for him, but he snaps at me.

Stay back, He growls
Esmeray, Stone warns, growling.
I hold up a hand.

Rejected Wolf

Let her help, brother, the one sitting beside me says.

She can't... Oni kills people. I'll be dead soon. She can't even understand us. How dare you call her our alpha? No female is ever alpha!

Shut the fuck up! She can!

The hurt one snaps at the one beside me, cursing him out.

"Stop it. I can help and I can hear!" I say, shaking. The injured one looks up at me. I reach down, touching his fur. "Calm down. I can help." I scoop him up in my arm, feeling his blood leak down my arms. He snaps, catching me shoulder with his sharp teeth. I wince, but I don't drop him. Instead, I stand, carrying him. "He's injured. Can we go back, Silver?"

Silver nods.

Stone shifts before me. "Let me take him."

I shake my head. I try my best not to look down at his dick. "Shift back. I doubt the girls will appreciate that."

"Are you sure? You're bleeding."

"I train for a reason."

Stone eyes me before nodding. He shifts back, guiding us back home. I carry the injured wolf all the way back, even if my arms shake and sweat runs down my forehead. As soon as we get the door open, I shout for Kira and Claire for help.

Liza peeks into the foyer. "Oh, god! Hang on! Take him to the guest room!"

212

I nod, even with a tired, shaking body, I carry him to the guest room and carefully set him on the bed.

"Who are these wolves?" Claire asks, touching the injured one.

He snaps at her, and I grab his jaw before he can hurt her, pushing him down. "Calm down, now!"

His chest is heaving, and his dark eyes meet mine. *Fuck you. I don't know you.*

"And yet, I risked my life to save your dumb ass so do *not* snap again," I order.

His dark eyes move away from me.

"Can... You can hear them?" Kira questions.

"They might be possible pack members."

Stone enters, putting on a shirt. Thank god he's dressed. "Why did you just run out of the house like that?"

"Because they needed my help. I heard them calling," I say, rubbing the injured one's head.

"Did another pack attack?" Claire asks. "Stone, have your mom bring water and towels. Lots. First Aid kit too. This one isn't healing as fast."

"A demonic wolf attacked them," I answer her first question.

Oni! The wolf next to me says.

I hesitate. *Is that what they were called?* "He said Oni," I correct.

"Oni means demon..." Kai says, entering. "What can I do?"

213

Rejected Wolf

"I need help because he's going to shift back for me to patch up," Claire says.

The injured wolf move uncomfortably. *No.*

I let out a sigh. "He doesn't seem to like us."

"Use your charm, E," Krew says with a handful of stuff.

I smirk a bit. "Thanks, Krew. Trying here. He's unphased."

I'll shift back. Just... cover me... the brother near the side of the bed says.

"Krew, hold up a towel for this wolf. He's going to shift first to show his brother we will not kill him."

Krew listens, handing me another towel before holding one up. Softly, I put it against the black wolf's ribs. He whines.

"I know. We are going to help." I whisper.

Behind me, I hear the realigning of bones, every crack as the guy shifts back. I am too nervous to look over. I have never seen another wolf naked besides my mates.

"What's your name?" Krew asks, making me turn just as the guy wraps the towel around his waist.

"Kylo," the soft velvety voice says, and I look at him. Like my men, Kylo is rippled with muscles. Tattoos cover his right arm, all the way down to his wrist but the other has only a few. He has a wolf tattooed against his chest and a moon against his throat. His abs are completely bare, leaving a deep v

214

that goes straight to his towel. He's skin is yellowish tan, showing off his Asian heritage. His hair is long and hanging down to his shoulder while his dark almond eyes look at me.

Oh fuck, do I look like shit?

My chest skips a beat as I pry my eyes from him to his injured brother. "See. No killing. Shift so we can help you."

"Listen to her, brother," Kylo says. "His name is Xave."

Xave. Great. He sounds hot. I can't deal with packmates being hot.

No.

I let out a sigh. "He's going to do it."

"Esmeray," Kai speaks softly, making me look back. His eyes are on Kylo's back. "He has the mark."

"Turn." I order.

Kylo listens, turning.

My eyes glance down at the back dimples he has and his strong lower back, right above his ass. But my eyes land on Kylo's shoulder. The wolf rune sits on his back. "He does. Xave, we are pack mates."

Prove it, Xave says.

"Krew, show him," I order. Krew listens. My eyes glide down his strong back. This is illegal. *The goddess hates me for sure.*

Show yours, Alpha.

I let out a frustrated growl. "Listen, you stubborn stubborn…" I take a deep breath. "Shift, so

215

you don't bleed out and die. I can't show you my rune because of a skin condition."

The shift is quick, making me now realize I was looking at an actual twin. His skin color is the same. His almond shaped eyes narrow on me. He has a piercing on his septum and a few scattered black tattoos. His not as strong as his brother, but just are fucking large and wide. *Handsome as well.* His thick black hair hangs down in a mess to his chest. His ribs have a gash in it from the Oni wolves, and his hand is fucked up as well. "Convenient, Alpha," he says sarcastically, pulling the blanket further up his hips.

"Fuck you." I groan, pressing the towel into his wound a bit more.

He winces with a hisses.

"Get the boys clothes," Silver says to someone.

I nod, looking everywhere but Xave's body. *How dare they be this hot? You're dying.*

"How did you hear them?" Kira asks, touching my hip.

I shrug.

"You can only communicate with packs if you're shifted too."

"Oh… I didn't know…"

"Do you know anything?" Xave asks, then he's hissing as Claire pours alcohol on his hand.

"That's what you get," I mutter. "Kira, take over."

She nods. We switch, and I push away, looking down at my bloody clothes. I feel a hand on my waist. "How's your shoulder?" Zeno asks.

I feel the spot that Xave bit me on. The marks are already gone. "Healed."

He nods.

"Good," Stone says. "We all need to talk, Esmeray."

I swallow. I don't like the sound of that.

Esmeray

"Did I... do something wrong?" I question as I glance around the room.

"No. I guess not." Stone puts his hands on his hips.

I raise a brow. "I know I pushed myself too hard and I'm sorry about that. I didn't mean to pass out and worry you all into coming here. But I'm okay."

He cocks a brow.

"How come you didn't tell us about Reed?" He asks.

I glance at Silver before glancing at Kai. "Huh? Did you go through my phone or something?"

218

"Do I need to?"

I almost laugh. "Okay. I'm confused. Stop being cryptic, Stone."

It's silent for a moment. I move to him in case he doesn't want to say it aloud. "He rejected you, didn't he?"

My heart drops. *How did he find out?* I open my mouth. *Should I lie?* "Did he tell you?"

"Why would I have to hear it from him?"

I shrug. "It's not a huge deal. We have more important things going on, like Xave dying."

"Don't pull me into this," Xave grumbles.

"Sorry..." I run a hand over my face with a sigh.

"You just passed out because of that dick head! What do you mean?" Stone raises his voice, and I deeply didn't appreciate that. I grab his shirt, pulling him out into the hall.

"I... I didn't think that all I felt was because of him. It's fine, now."

"Fine?! Esmeray. You didn't tell us either. This is something you tell your pack as an alpha. This is something you tell your mate!"

I swallow hard. "Why would I tell you that? So, you guys can beat him up?"

"Yes!" he shouts.

"I was doing what was right for the pack and trying to get him back, so you guys didn't feel what I fucking felt!"

"This is not something you bare alone!"

I roll my eyes. "How do I tell you that your best friend rejected you because you had a shared mate or female alpha?! He didn't just reject me, Stone. He rejected you, Kai, Krew and Zeno. How was I supposed to tell you guys that?"

He snorts, rolling his blue eyes. "I would rather know. Thanks, Alpha."

I clench my fist, rage surging. "*Fuck* you."

He rolls his eyes. "You don't tell us shit, do you? Do you even trust us? We are your pack and your mates, and you can't tell us something like that?"

I swallow as tears fill my eyes. "You know that answer."

"Do I?"

"Shut up!" Kai snaps at us. "Why are you fighting over this? If anything, this is Reed's fault!"

My hands shake as I push past Stone and move into my room. I don't slam the door, but I do lock it. I need to take a quick shower and change. Xave's blood still covers my body.

How could I let it get this bad?

After showering and changing, I move from my bedroom feeling comfortable at least. Claire steps out of the other room, just as I do. She gives me a sad smile.

"How are they?" I ask.

"They are good. Xave is healing now and seems to be doing better than we could have asked for. No fever or symptoms of the poison."

I nod. "Good, that's amazing."

Claire nods and lowers her voice when she says, "The only way to feel better, Esmeray, is cutting ties with Reed."

I let out a sigh. "Like everyone does? This is what he's used to. His dad gave up on him, and his mother doesn't care. Why would I be the next person? He doesn't... deserve that, no matter how much he's hurt me. Right?" *I hated Reed. I hated what he's doing to this pack, and we've barely spoken.*

"If he wanted to change, he would have already."

I nod. "Thanks... for everything."

"When you are ready with what you choose, let me know."

I nod again, rounding her before moving to the guest room.

Kylo stands, fully clothed now. "Hey..."

"Hi."

"Is it true? Those guys are all your mates?"

"Sadly." I move inside the room. "I have five, but Reed is rejecting me."

Xave sucks his teeth. "Heard the whole thing, koneko. We know."

I raise a brow. "What did you call me? Also, what is an Oni again?"

He shrugs, making me look at Kylo. "Oni is a demon in Japanese. We are both Japanese, so... And those things look like demons."

"And the other word he says?" I ask.

He shrugs, cheeks flushing a bit. "I have more questions."

I nod for him to go on.

"How did you become the alpha of this group?"

"Uh... I didn't know what shifters were a few months ago. I just felt the pull when they came searching for me. I've never shifted in my life, so it was very weird to be an alpha."

His dark pulls pull together, drawing my attention to his deep brown eyes. "Your parents didn't tell you what you were?"

I smile sadly. "I don't know my mother, but my father died when I was thirteen. Neither of them left me a note on all these terms."

He nods. "And we usually first shift at fifteen or sixteen... I understand. First female alpha since the Goddess, huh?"

I nod. "Amazing, right? Our goal is to get me to shift so we can stay in the Moon Born academy."

"Can't be too hard, huh?"

I shrug. "Apparently. Because now I'm juggling new pack members while juggling trying to shift and deal with mates." And yet here I am, wanting them both as mates. "How did you guys get close to here? I saw you guys a month ago."

Kylo nods. "We felt the same pull and came here from New York. We stayed at a motel nearby until those akuma no ōkami came after us. The demon wolves... So now we are here."

"This is Stone's parents' house and I'm sure we can figure something out for you guys to stay…"

"The mate that was just yelling at you?" Xave asks, chuckling.

I shrug. "He's stressed. He's never like that. A lot is happening in such a short time. He is usually very calm."

"Oh, I can tell," Xave says, putting his arms behind his head, looking at me.

I send him a glare. "You just want to get punched, huh?"

"Sure, koneko. Try me," he dares.

"What does that mean?"

He shrugs. "Figure it out."

I scoff, looking at Kylo. "Your brother is very lovely."

Kylo chuckles. "Don't mind him. He's used to being a lone wolf. He doesn't do well with authority. I'm the better twin."

I cock a brow, smiling lightly. *Twins... Can I have another pair of twins? Two with two different personalities. Kylo seems to be the kinder twin, while Xave is on edge. Rightfully so.*

Rejected Wolf

"Fuck, don't you have enough mates?" Xave groans and I snap my eyes from his brother. "Go stare at one of them, weirdo."

I scoff. "Whatever. Are you guys hungry or thirsty?"

Kylo shakes his head.

"Do you guys need anything? I'm sure we can get you into a separate room, so you don't have to listen to Xave's mouth."

Kylo smirks. "No. We are okay. It'll probably be better, so I can keep an eye on him."

I nod. "Have a good night. I'm two doors down, so let me know if you guys need anything."

"Thanks, Esmeray," Kylo says, making me look back at him. I didn't even know he knew my name until now. I smile softly, nodding and closing the door behind me.

Zeno comes out of Krew's guest room, and I meet him halfway in the hall. "Hi."

He wraps his arms around me, kissing my temple. "Go get some sleep, Mami." Without another word, he moves to his room.

I swallow, waiting a minute before popping into Krew's room. He's sitting on the bed talking to Kai who is standing. Both look up at me.

"On a scale one to ten, how much do you guys hate me?" I ask, looking down.

"Zero," Kai says while Krew says, "Too much."

I look at Krew but see that goofy boyish grin on his lips. "Come here, baby."

Slowly, I move to him, but once I get close enough, he pulls me into his lap, wrapping his arms around me. I nuzzle my face into his neck.

"Why didn't you tell us?"

"Do you know how embarrassing it is to have someone reject you and his best friends because of you? I didn't think he actually did it, until..." I trail off.

Krew let out a sigh. "Well, the way he's been acting, I'd rather not have him around me."

I pull back, looking up at him. "You are just going to reject him that easily?"

Krew nods. "Fuck him. No one treats my girl like shit, besides me."

I snort. "Thanks, Krew. But won't you feel bad?"

He shakes his head. "I doubt I will. He started a fight with us when I was fucking dying."

Kai touches my back. "I think I'm with Krew on this one."

His hazel eyes look down at me while I twist to see more of him. "How could you guys just decide that?"

"Because we don't want people to treat us like shit. You shouldn't either. You really think you're going to forgive him?"

I blink. *Am I?*

Rejected Wolf

I reach into my pocket, pulling out my phone before pulling up his conversations. "He's... seeing someone else."

Krew takes the phone and looks at all the pictures. More were sent after that day. "His ex, Jess... Is this why you were so upset on Sunday? They sent you this shit?"

I shrug. "I missed you guys too..."

Krew passes the phone to Kai who curses. "Stupid fucker. These are recent too, because I know she just dyed her hair blonde."

"How long ago did they break up?"

"A year ago. Reed cheated."

I snort. "How cute."

Kai throws the phone on the bed. It bounces a few times before settling. "You don't deserve something like that, Esme."

Krew nods, peppering kisses across my neck. "He's the weakest link, and honestly, he's weighing you down. You are so unhappy."

I let out a sigh. "I just didn't want to be another person who gave up on him."

"That's a choice he made himself." Krew pulls me close. "Come on, you look tired." He stands, holding me in his arms before literally throwing me on the bed and letting me bounce like the phone.

I let out a giggle as Krew crawls onto the bed.

"Have a good night," Kai says.

"Wait!" I sit up, looking at Krew. "Can he stay?"

Krew snorts. "No. Fuck him." I hit his shoulder, making him chuckle. "Yeah.... he can stay."

"You can say no," I offer.

He shakes his head, curls falling against his forehead. "It'll be amazing to sandwich you. Maybe you'll forget about that douchebag."

I snort, opening my hand for Kai. He smiles warmly before turning off the lights and crawling under the covers with us. Both twins have one side of me. Krew sits up, shedding out of his shirt before pulling me close.

I run a hand up his chest, resting on it.

Kai moves close, wrapping an arm around me and pressing his hips into my back. *He's not hard...* *Sad.* I wiggle my ass until he's hard against my back and panting in my ear.

"Better. Good night," I mutter.

"Asshole," Kai mutters into my shoulder.

Krew snorts.

I didn't think I was as tired as I thought I was until I fell asleep quickly to both of their calm breathing.

Esmeray

The best way to wake up is sandwiched between two annoyingly hot twins, and I'm not talking about the sweating heat I'm feeling against my skin.

My eyes flutter open to see Kai on his back, his arm in place of my pillow. His white hair is a perfect mess, and his face looks peaceful. Twisting, I see Krew now facing me. His mouth is open and he's drooling a bit on his hand. I giggle softly. My breath on his face must have stirred him because he scrunches his nose like someone has rubbed a feather on it. His mouth closes and one of his sleepy eyes opens.

Biting my lip, I try to close my eyes, so he can't see I'm awake.

He shifts closer to me, whispering, "God, Esmeray is always drooling on me. Gross girl."

I snicker. "I did not. You drooled on yourself."

He leans in, kissing my dry lips. I pull back wetting them before going back in for another kiss.

"Morning," I mutter, pushing my hips into his. Our cores line up perfectly and he's hard from the morning.

His hand grabs my waist as he inhales sharply. "Fuck, don't tease me."

I push him onto his back, climbing on top of him and straddling his hips. His hard dick sits right against my heated core. I reach up, taking off my t-shirt and throwing it to the floor.

His eyes move over my bare breasts. "Please don't tease me. We don't have to do this, if you don't want to."

I lean down, rubbing my core against him and kissing his neck. "But I really, *really* want to. I want you, Krew." *I think he's earned it too.* He showed me how much he's changed from his mistake. Plus, I've realized we weren't together, and we didn't know we were mates when he was with that girl.

He grunts, grabbing me and flipping us so he's on top of me. His lips roam my neck then my chest, making my head fall backward. He takes a moment before flicking my hard nipple with his tongue before moving downward again.

My breathing is heavy as his hand slips into my pants. I lift my hips, letting him take them off. His eyes scan over the lacy white triangle over my pussy.

"Oh, these are staying on." His breath makes me shudder as it hits my pussy. I can't even remember the last time I've been eaten out. *It was with Kai.*

I feel watchful eyes on me, making me look over. Kai watches us, comfortably. His eyes meet mine. I lean forward just as Krew pushes aside my thong. I connect my lips with Kai as Krew runs his tongue through my folds. Pleasure rushes through me as a wave. I moan out into Kai's mouth, which makes him kiss me harder.

Krew fully puts his warm mouth on my clit, licking and nibbling on it with no real pattern, but so much skill. I roll my hips, grabbing Kai's hand and pulling it on my breast. He kneads it, rolling the nipple between his fingers.

Kai swallows each of my moans.

Krew's fingers play with my slit as his tongue still wiggles against my clit.

"Oh, fuck! Please, Krew!" I pull back just to moan that.

Kai's head moves down to take my nipple into his hot wet mouth as Krew plunges two fingers inside of me.

I arch a bit, whimpering. "Dear god!"

Krew's fingers work on me skillfully rubbing the top of my walls. It makes me squirm and writhe under their touches. His other hand grips my waist, trying to hold me down. But one hand won't do.

As Kai fucking knew, his hand grabs my other side, holding me firmly still.

Krew drives me wild, fucking my pussy with his fingers as his tongue eggs me to the edge.

Kai switches nipples, pinching the wet one with his free hand.

Pleasure overwhelms me as I wiggle and try to fuck Krew's face. I try everything, begging for them to let me go. But they don't listen.

So, I do the only thing I can. I reach down and softly grasp Kai's dick. He grunts, filling with a swirl of heat. I rub his dick a few times before shoving my hand in his pants and rubbing it more.

Krew slams his fingers into my pussy hard, earning a cry from me.

The pressure builds, tightening my hips and suddenly I don't want them to stop. I don't want to be fucked. I want to finish.

My free hand grabs Krew's hair and I moan out. "Don't stop, Krew. Please!" I rub Kai's precum into his shaft a bit faster. I clench a fist into Krew's head. "Holy fuck! I'm so close." The orgasm is rising in me as I try to catch my breath and squirm. *I want to fuck his face. I need more pressure there.*

231

Rejected Wolf

Krew's fingers begin to curl faster, making me cry out.

I grab the sheets, twisting my head as the orgasm hits me like a train. I moan so loud, I think someone might hear us. Throwing my head back and arching, I finally come undone and can breathe. "Fuck." I mutter.

Krew licks his face and fingers. "Mhm, you taste so good."

I groan, closing my shaking thighs.

"Hands and knees, baby."

I move, rolling over. Kai shreds his clothes, getting in front of me while Krew gets behind me. I lean forward, wiggling my ass, as my tongue runs up Kai's dick, tasting the salty precum.

Crack!

I whine from the spank Krew gives me. I didn't even know he had gotten naked until I felt his tip running through my folds. I glance back, holding Kai's dick in my hands. I catch a glimpse of Krew rubbing his long, thick cock before sliding it in. It slides in so easily and painlessly, making me moan.

Facing Kai, I meet his eyes as I lean forward to kiss the tip before swirling my tongue around it. Kai closes his eyes, groaning.

Krew pulls out before slamming into me. It pushes me to take Kai all the way down my throat. And when I gag, Krew fucking laughs at me.

I push back against him, slurping up the drool from Kai's cock.

Again, Krew begins fucking me hard. Every time he pushes inside of me, I take Kai's cock in my throat and then when he pulls back, I do too.

Kai's hand fists my hair and holds my chin with the other. He follows the rhythm, slamming himself harshly in my throat over and over.

Although it hurts and drool is running down my chin, it makes my pussy pulse and tighten around Krew.

I gargle a moan, gripping the sheets. This turns me on so much that it's bringing another orgasm closer and closer.

Krew grabs my hips and slams hard into me and when he pulls back, I tighten around him. "Oh, fuck."

I moan hard, bouncing.

Kai's fist tightens in my hair as he groans.

Would it be possible to all come at the same time? That would be so amazing.

I grab Kai's shaft, bob my head faster and I move my hips faster on Krew. Fuck if they don't come soon, I'm going to come alone.

Krew spanks my ass hard. "Keep going, baby."

Like I'd fucking stop.

I move faster, moaning over and over. The orgasm is coming faster than I want. But both men grip my body and fuck me so erratically. I pull my mouth off Kai and moan, pumping his dick hard.

"I'm so close, baby," Krew says.

My eyes move up to Kai, who is moaning so loud. His eyes are closed, and his brows are pulled together with focus. He's going to come.

I keep my pace. "Please, don't stop. Fuck, Krew! I'm gonna come." I shove Kai back down my throat and try to make him come.

"Come for me, baby," Krew says in his husky voice, fingers digging into my hips.

My thighs shake with the impending orgasm riding in my hips.

But Kai comes first, pushing himself in my throat tightly and filling my throat until I'm choking. He pulls back, panting and moaning.

Krew's fingers find and rub the swollen nub. I cry out, grabbing the sheets. Kai pushes my head into the sheets and holds my hands behind my back. Krew grabs one of my wrists and begins fucking me harder than I've ever been. It sends me over the edge, and I cry his name over and over again. I hit cloud nine, squeezing my eyes closed.

"Fuck!" Krew growls, riding until I hit my peak and stiffen. He comes hard and hot inside of me, rubbing my ass lightly until I'm done twitching.

"Fuck," I mutter, rolling and laying down.

"I need a shower," Krew says.

Kai nods. "But Stone's mother is making French toast."

How does he know that? I inhale, smelling the sweet cinnamon and aromatic thick bread she uses. "Oh shit… Quick shower. Someone get me clothes."

Krew rolls his eyes. "Feral for French toast."

"If she does the fucking sticks," I say. "I'd literally come again."

Kai shoots up. "I'll make sure she does."

I snort and dance my way to the kitchen after a shower with Krew. The sweet smell of dopamine makes me smile. *Nothing can ruin that.*

"You and your relationship with food," Ivory snorts, moving around me.

That, and I just realized Krew and I just mated and built our bond. I feel so good.

"Hi, Esmeray." A voice makes me look up.

Reed sits at the table with Zeno, Claire and Kira.

Heat runs down my body, shaking me to my core. I look at Kira. *Warn a fucking bitch.* I just give a nod, twisting around to leave. *French toast is not worth a heartache.*

I bump straight into Xave's hard chest.

"Watch it, *koneko*." Xave grumbles. I glance up before nodding and moving around him and disappearing behind the wall. He leans back to look at me. "What's wrong?"

Rejected Wolf

I look up at him. *Why does he care? Does he actually even care?* But his dark eyes are soft for the first time meeting me. I swallow my nerves. "Glad... Glad you're okay. No fever or... anything."

He nods, eyes moving back to the dining room. "Is that... Reed, I'm guessing?"

I look up at his almost black eyes before nodding.

"He looks like a bitch." His eyes dart up and down Reed.

I let out a huff of laughter as he walks into the dining room. Stone walks down the stairs with Kylo. His icy blue eyes land right on me and it makes my heart pound more. "What's..." Stone starts, brows pulling together.

We are fighting, right? He doesn't care. My eyes water.

Stone peeks in the kitchen, stopping Kylo. Stone makes a grumble noise. "Fucking ass is actually here..."

I look up at Kylo. He's just as tall as Stone and just as wide. "Thank god. Xave is good."

Kylo nods.

Stone grabs my face, directing my attention to him. "Say the word, Alpha, and I will beat his ass."

I want to laugh, but I also want to see Reed get beaten up. *But I want to be the one to beat him up.* "He's seeing someone else, Stone." It comes out in a small whisper.

Stone's face softens and he let out a sigh.

"She sent me pictures of them kissing and stuff. Do you know how embarrassing that is? I feel like a stupid teenager again," I admit.

"You're not stupid. You're too kind and fuckers like that take advantage of it." Stone kisses my head.

I look up, getting lost in the sky-blue eyes he has. "No more fighting. Not today. I need you as my beta and my support."

He nods. "I'm sorry I yelled at you. It's more of… I hate that I can't protect you."

I punch his shoulder softly. "Please. You'll know when I need protection."

"If anything counts," Kylo says. "I don't like the sound of the guy and I can already tell you deserve better and *have* better. Seems like you have your whole pack behind you and they'll do anything for you."

I smile softly. "Yeah, I do. No fighting, and let's hope I shift soon."

Stone turns to lead the way but stops before holding out his hand. *I'm the alpha. I should go first.* Hand in hand, we walk into the dining room. I lift my chin, feeling slightly stronger with my pack behind me. Kylo pulls out my chair and he goes to sit with Xave and Zeno.

Reed and I meet eyes.

Before I can think of what to say, Silver walks in. "Ah, Reed, so good for you to *finally* join us once."

Rejected Wolf

I bit my lip to keep from making a face and bursting into laughter. I glance at Krew who makes a face at me. *Fucker. He's trying to get me to laugh.* I lick my lips and clear my throat.

"Thanks, Silver. Who are these two?" Reed points to Xave who glares at him.

"Meet Xave and his twin, Kylo. They are a part of the pack."

"Twins…" Krew mutters. "There's only room for one set, sorry, guys."

I kick him under the table and send him a look.

"I was kidding! Maybe," he says with a smirk creeping on his lips.

I roll my eyes. I like when he's not pissed at Reed. Maybe he feels just as good with the bond.

"Are they mates, too?" Reed snaps.

I raise a brow, feeling so much stronger in front of my pack. "They just joined last night, *Reed*."

His jaw tightens.

"I'm gonna see if mom needs help," Ivory says, pulling Kira to the kitchen doors.

I wait for Reed to call me a whore to make fun of me. *Would he?* I stand, moving to the kitchen. "Same." I step in the kitchen. "Hey, Liza," I say, looking at Stone's mom who is covered in powdered sugar.

"How bad is the tension?" Liza asks.

"Bad." I giggle.

238

"So, fucking bad." Kira bursts into laughter. "Also, I did warn you. Answer your phone instead of sleeping with the twins."

Ivory gasps. "You slept with Xave and Kylo, already?"

"No! I slept in Krew's room with Kai and Krew and we did nothing." I send Kira a look.

"Sure. Why do you think we got soundproofed rooms?" Liza jokes.

"Can we just talk about how hot the new twins are?" Ivory says dreamily.

An inch of jealousy enters me, but nothing horrible. *They'd never date you.*

"They both seem very interested in you." Kira bumps me.

I roll my eyes. "Kylo is just nice. Xave hates me."

"Then why is he calling you kitten in Japanese?"

I gasp. "What?! Is that what he's saying? I feel like he's using it more as an insult than cute pet nickname."

"Do you have a pull with the other twins?" Ivory gasps.

My eyes widen and I look at Liza who seems like she doesn't care and is more intrigued than anything. "I hope not... I mean, no. I have four and I think that's enough."

Rejected Wolf

"You are living every girl's dream and you think that's enough?" Liza says, pointing her fork at me. She makes me laugh.

Esmeray

No one—and I mean no one—could kill my mood. French toast sticks are my entire life. My father used to make them for me every Sunday morning. It's the first food Stone made me and it's the best thing that I've ever had. I'm not a shitty cook but I just can't do it like they do.

"Are you going to marry French toast?" Xave says, drawing my attention. I am dancing, and for some reason, he decides to interrupt me.

"Maybe, *koneko*. Just maybe. French toast doesn't talk back."

He sends a glare.

Rejected Wolf

"Do you like it more than you love me?" Krew asks, looking down.

"For sure. French toast is above it all. My dad used to make it every Sunday and it tasted exactly like this." I shrug, going back to eating.

"Maybe my mom will finally give us the recipe," Ivory says.

Liza snorts. "No! Vixen got it from a family friend."

I shrug. "My father never told me either."

After eating and cleaning up, Reed touches my bicep. "Can we talk, Esmeray?" His eyes move to Stone who is by my side. "*Alone.*"

Stone snorts.

"No. We talk as a pack," I answer, pulling from him. *I deserve better, like my mates said.* "What you have to say, they can hear now."

Reed rolls his eyes. "Listen, I'm sorry, I…"

I bounce my brow. His eyes move to Stone as if he's scared that he might hurt Reed. "Rejected me as a mate, alpha and pack member? While I was currently dying because of the demon wolves."

Kylo's eyes widen.

Rage runs down my chest, but it's not mine… *Are these my mates' feelings?*

"Yes. I acted irrationally."

I glance at Kira and Silver who sit nearby, pretending not to listen.

"But I have reasons. I want to make this work and I want to take my rejection back."

Krew fucking snorts behind me, making me laugh. Fuck. I feel so much stronger with four mates and two packmates behind me. It feels nice for them to know the whole truth and back me up.

"Oh, shut it!" Reed snaps, making me raise my brows. "I'm serious."

Kai shifts, wanting to say something, but I think I know what he's going to say. *Say it... Say what you want.*

"Who is Jess?"

Reed's face drains of color. "Uh... She's an ex."

"Doesn't look like an ex in the pictures and video she sent me." We lock eyes, his filled with fear or regret. I can't tell.

Poor Kylo shifts uncomfortably beside me. He and Xave got thrown into this. They don't even need to be here for this. They have no idea what's going on.

"She sent you pictures?"

I nod. "You know... I don't think you're sincere on what you're saying, maybe that's because I don't trust a single word that comes out of your mouth. You called me a whore. You watched me almost get beaten up, then rejected me when I was torn to shreds. You've never protected me as a mate or a member. You've always hated me. Hey, that's probably because you now have to listen to a *whore* talk. I don't..." I shrug, looking up at him. Part of me was torn about how I feel. I wanted to make this work but if Krew and Kai can so easily drop someone like that... Especially, someone they knew longer, I can do this. I don't need Reed. I have Zeno, Stone, Kai, and Krew. They make me realize I do deserve better. "I want to reject you as a mate."

His eyes widen.

"Now, as an alpha and pack member, it's not fully up to me because I'm not the only one you rejected there. It will be up to the guys if we should forgive you and trust you to have our back in the pack."

It's silent for a moment.

"They don't have to decide yet, because four of them are your best friends. Two of them really don't have a good impression on you. I say we relax today and decide later." I turn to move away, but Reed grabs my wrist.

Rage seeps from his eyes as he glares at me. "I know the truth. I know what you did to him."

I rip my wrist from him. "What?"

"Dan Cloverman."

"Who?" I question. The name really doesn't ring a bell in my head.

But Silver stands and shouts, "That's enough!" I twist to see Stone's father's eyes filled with rage. I've never seen him this mad before. *Does he know that name?*

"You helped her! I know the truth of what you did to him." Reed shouts back.

I blink. "What the fuck are you talking about, Reed?"

"You're Ernie Devine's daughter, aren't you?! She's hiding more shit!" he snaps in my face.

That's when Silver hits the table. "Reed! Stop it." I stare at Reed until he finally storms out of the room. It's silent for a moment.

My hands are shaking at the outburst, but I'm not sure why. *Reed knows my father's name. Ernie. But why didn't he tell me he knew the name?*

I snort, running a hand through my hair. "Welcome to the pack," I say to the two new pack members before moving from the room and going upstairs. *How dysfunctional do we have to be before Kylo and Xave decided to leave? Because... if I were them, I would have left already.*

Kira follows after me and leads me up the stairs to my room. Once inside, she closes the door behind us. I throw myself down on the bed.

"Was that your dad's name?"

I glance over. "Ernie? Yes, but I don't know the Dan guy."

"Then I wouldn't worry too much about it..."

Confusion runs through me, making me pull my brows together. "Silver seems to know who he is, and it seems to have set him off... I don't understand why being Alpha is so fucking hard. I want to cry, and I want to give up."

"It doesn't have to be."

I snort at her answer.

"I haven't seen you all month, E. Let's have some fun." She bumps me, smirking.

"Fun?! The twins are this close to leaving." I pinch my fingers together.

"So, let's drink and let's have some fun."

I smirk. "Kira."

She grabs my arm. "Come on! You know you want to!" She shakes me. "Please, Esmeray! Let's forget there are six hot boys in the house and just swim and drink."

"Is drowning involved?" I deadpan. This isn't what we should be doing, especially when I have so many questions in my head.

She snorts, moving to the closet. She moves through it until she finds a white bathing suit. "Who bought you this?!"

"You just want a reason to drink. You know I almost died and Xave almost died and here we are thinking about drinking."

She snorts and repeats herself. "Who bought you this?"

"Krew! He likes white and it happens to look good as *fuck* on me."

She throws it at me. "Wear it."

"Well... I have that skin condition."

She raises a brow. "You've never cared before."

"I just don't want to be a target for Reed or in case Kylo sees."

Her jaw drops with a gasp. "You like him!"

I shake my head.

"I promise you if you wear this, he'll drool. You're hot, Esmeray. Since when do we care about Reed and his dumb opinions."

When he calls you a whore everyday...?

She glances over. "At least you're a sexy whore, koneko!"

I throw myself on the bed with a smile. *Oh god.*

It takes Kira a half an hour to convince me that I deserve the time to relax and have fun. The swimsuit is just as scandalous as the first one that Stone's mother made me wear. It's a one piece, though the sides are cut out and the stomach, leaving a v shape. The top is held together—and up—by a gold chain. It's very cheeky, but it fits comfortably. I put a non-see-through cover up on before sliding on white sandals.

"You're lucky I'm talking to someone, or I swear I'd be a better mate than half of the guys," Kira says.

I roll my eyes, chuckling. "Yeah, okay. I think Krew got me this for the ass cut out."

"At least he can do something right," Kira adds, making me laugh.

Rejected Wolf

She's just wearing a black bikini, but unlike me, she's not trying to get attention. She leads the way down the stairs to the living room. Krew and Zeno sit with Kylo, where they are playing video games. I roll my eyes. Stone looks up, ceasing his talking to Kai and his sister. "What are you guys doing?"

I shrug. "Nothing." Xave pops a brow at me. I move to Silver's office, knocking. I hear short movement behind the doors before they open. He looks down at me. "Hey, Sil. Can I have your keys to the bar?"

He bounces a brow. "You know me, letting you have the key to condone an underage girl to become an alcoholic."

I snicker. "I won't say shit. I promise. Look!" I cover my eyes and hold out my hand.

He chuckles. "Don't go wild and don't drink my shit."

"Yes, sir." I smile sweetly, taking the keys from his hands. I smile softly before moving away. He closes his door and I move out of the living room.

"Wait!" Krew stops me.

I twist and look up.

"You're going swimming?"

"Mhm."

He smirks. "What color bathing suit are you wearing?"

I bit away my smile, but it seeps through. *How can this little goofy fucker make me smile so much?*

"Hint: it matches my toes." I step away from the living room.

"I'm coming!" Krew shouts.

Thud.

I giggle, knowing poor Krew defiantly fell. I look up at Kira who is waiting at the door for me. "Ass!" Kai says, punching him. "Watch it!"

I share a look with Kira as we giggle.

Kira grabs the towels and sets up the speaker outside as I unlock the closet that holds the liquor right by the backdoor and bathroom. I move through the shelves, grabbing some wine, beer and wine coolers. Walking out and gasping, I almost collide with Kylo.

"Shit!" Kylo says. He catches one of the bottles before it can smash against the ground.

I smile. "Here, hold this." I hand off the wine and wine coolers. "Are you swimming?"

"Uh. I guess."

"Like beer?"

He nods.

I grab another case out of the million that are there. *How old is he? Will his parents be okay with him drinking? Where are his parents?* "Hey, Ky?"

"Ky?" He cocks a brow, smirking.

I bounce a brow. "Don't like my nicknames, huh?"

He smiles. "No, it's fine, but no one calls me that."

Rejected Wolf
"Perfect. What... do your parents think about you being here from New York?"

He clears his throat as I lead out to the back where the table and pools are. "They, uh, are dead. But if they were alive, I'm sure they would hate it, even if we are twenty. Mother was always very protective over us…"

I nod. "Sorry for your loss."

"You, too."

I hold out my hands for him to hand over the bottles as we got to the door.

"I got it. I'll change in a second," he says.

I lead the way out and set down the boxes on the table. "Will you do me a favor? Give these keys to Stone?"

He nods.

I pull it away before he can grab them. "I'm trusting you, Ky."

He smiles. "You can trust me, Es."

His voice is heavy and husky. My eyes glance at his lips. There's a pull between us, well at least on my end. I lick my lips, handing over the keys. His fingers brush against mine and it made me heat up a bit. *How dare he makes me feel like a schoolgirl?*

He takes the keys, and I watch his round ass and muscular back a bit as he leaves.

Music plays loudly through the speaker, making me jolt. I glance over at Kira, seeing her smile. It's a Spanish pop song. I can't hold back my hips as I pull out a wine cooler and crack it before handing it to her. Then popping another for me, singing the Spanish lyrics.

This is a song Zeno and I danced to in the club.

I sip my wine cooler, knowing I can drink like six of these and barely feel a buzz. I like to switch between beer and this. I kick off my sandals, ready to jump in with this blazing sun coming down on me. It's been a while since we've swam together. Last time, Moon Born was still up and running.

"Did I miss it?!" Krew shouts. It makes me twist around to see my four mates all staring at me from near the door. "Go on. Take it off."

I roll my eyes, grabbing the hem of my cover dress and pulling it up and over my head. My hair falls against my bare back, and I look up. I see lust deep in each of their eyes, I even notice Xave staring a bit. I do a full spin, posing to show off my ass.

"Damn, you're so hot," Krew says, moving and scooping me up before the others can. He lays kisses against my neck, and I try to break free.

"Let me go! You're going to throw me in!"

He smiles, pulling back. "How did you know?"

"No!" is all I can scream before he jumps into the pool with me in his arms. He lets me go, letting me swim back to the surface. I push my hair back, just as Krew breaks to the surface, I splash him. "Ass!"

Krew swims to the shallow end before shedding his wet shirt and throwing it to the side of the pool. My eyes take in his bare chest before thinking, *I need my drink.*

I move to the front of the pool, climbing up the steps. The backdoor opens right as I step out, making me look up.

Kylo's eyes widen as he looks down at my body.

Nip slip? I glance down. Surprisingly those small triangles are in place. "Something wrong?"

He pries his eyes away. "No... Nope." He moves to the rest of the guys.

An old 2000s song comes on, making Kira and I meet eyes. We created this playlist together and it's a mixture of old and new songs. I move to the table that I set my drink on. "Are you coming?" I say to Stone pointing at the water.

Kai nods. "Close to it…" Eyes on my breasts. He's a boob guy, now. I throw a towel at his head. "Oh, sorry."

Stone puts his hand on my lower back right before rubbing my ass. "We will. Go swim with Krew."

I gag. "No. Z?"

Zeno looks up from my body. "Huh? Yeah, I'll come." He stands and sheds out of his shirt with one hand. My eyes run down to his happy trail.

What is with these hot men? I glance away, taking a gulp of my drink. I don't need to get turned on.

"How cold is it?"

"Not at all!" Krew shouts.

"He was talking to me!" I shout back. I turn to Z, touching his shoulder. "Not cold at all."

Zeno rolls his eyes, moving to the edge. "I bet it's fucking cold."

Stone scoffs, standing and kicking Zeno into the pool.

I chuckle, watching my mate resurface and push his hair back. I love when his black hair is down.

"Go, before I push your fat ass in the pool," he grumbles, near my ear. I can't lie. It turns me on, sending a swirl to my stomach.

"Fat ass, as in... I have a fat ass, or I am a fat ass?" I question.

"Both," Stone says, smacking my ass hard.

I hiss at the pain, pushing him. "Fucker! Stop, we have children around."

"Krew's fine."

I smirk, setting the drink at the edge before jumping in near Zeno. When I resurface, his hand wraps around my waist and pulls me close. I push his hair out of his face. "On a scale of one to ten, how fat am I?"

He rolls his eyes. "Stone's an asshole. You just *really* love food…"

I giggle and wrap my body around him, trying to drown us. He breaks free easily, throwing me over his shoulder like I weigh nothing. I come back up, pushing my hair back. "Hey! Wait until I can sling your ass everywhere!"

Krew wraps his arms around me from behind. Kira swims to us, rolling her brown eyes. "I always feel like I'm third wheeling."

I push away from Krew's arms. "I'll hold you, baby."

She splashes me. "No!"

Esmeray

I sit down at the table, giggling as Stone throws Kylo in the pool. Glancing over, I see Xave reclining back with a beer. "Are you coming in?" I question sweetly.

He cocks a brow. "No."

"Can you swim?"

He rolls his eyes. "Yes, koneko. I can swim."

"Why do you keep calling me kitten?"

He raises a brow again. "Figured it out, huh? It fits you, you're so… tiny and innocent."

I snort, grabbing a beer. "Far from innocent. I fuck four guys daily."

He shrugs.

"We like, fuck, *fuck*. Like very kink stuff." I imply.

"I don't care," he deadpans.

"I do. I'm not innocent."

A noise escapes his throat. "Okay, Esmeray."

I roll my eyes. *I don't know why I want him to go back to calling me Kitten. I have enough mates. Four? Is that enough for me or do I always need more? Kylo and Xave can't be my mates. If I want another mate, I could always accept Reed.* My chest aches at the thought of doing that. *Why would I want to forgive someone who treated me like that? Am I really that weak?*

Then I am making my pack decide if we want to accept him. I know Krew and Kai didn't, and probably not Stone. But Reed was best friends with Zeno more than anyone else. Does he want him to stay?

Xave stands, shredding his shirt. "All right, let's go."

I blink. "Huh?" I look at his strong tattooed chest, eyes running to his abs and slight 'v' running into his pants. I can faintly see the outline of his cock. "Huh?" His wound from the Oni wolf is all healed, faster than anyone else.

"You wanted me to swim, right?" He holds out his hand. "I don't need your mates thinking I made you sad."

I blink. *How does he know I was sad, even though I'm not really? I'm just thinking a lot.* I slide my hands into his, letting his warmth cradle me as I look up at him. This is the nicest he's been so far. He pulls me flush against his chest, drawing a gasp from my throat, before leaning down and throwing me over his shoulders. "Oh, my God! Let me down!" He doesn't listen, stepping into the deep end like he was walking normally. But he holds onto me, pulling me from his shoulder and carrying me to the surface. I gasp, pushing my hair back. "Ass! I could have died!"

He cocks a brow. "What? You can't swim? Someone get her before I let her drown."

Zeno fucking laughs as the fucking giant hands me off to him like I weight nothing. "Oh! I'm sick of men."

"Me too," Kira adds.

I swim on my back toward her. "Mhm, not tired of Valentin."

"That's because she is a *she*. Not a stinky man." I smile.

Krew paddles to me as I float on the surface. "Am I stinky, E?"

"No. Not at all, Krew." I smile at him.

He leans down and kisses my lips sideways. "Men are better than women any day."

I snort. "I have four men wrapped around my finger. Not the other way around," I tease. I don't think they are wrapped around my finger at all.

"Throw her," Xave suggests, making me scramble to get up right. I send him a glare.

257

"Stone!" I swim to him, wrapping my legs around him. He lounges his arms on the edge of the pool, keeping himself afloat. I tilt my head, innocently. "Can we order out and watch movies tonight?"

He cocks a brow. "I'm the example for being wrapped around your finger, aren't I?"

I gasp, touching my chest. "How low do you think of me? I was thinking about this all day. Ask Kira."

Kira nods, red dreads almost hitting the water. "You know her and food. She thought about it right after breakfast."

I nod. "Yes, I did."

Stone smirks. "Are you ever satisfied?"

My eyes drop to his lips, and I smile, tongue flicking to wet mine.

He rolls his blue eyes, wrapping his arms around me. "What do you want?"

I shrug. "You guys can pick. I'm never picky for food. Food is food to me."

He chuckles, deeply rumbling against my chest. "I know, E."

We all spend the next few hours talking around the small bar or swimming. It did feel nice to forget everything, even if it's only for a bit. Kylo seems to blend right in with Krew and Zeno, joking about the games and sports they liked. He gets me to laugh a few times too, and he seems to have a proud smirk when he hears me giggle. Xave took a bit to get him to warm up. He sat away from us, but I actively included him. I gave him beers and asked him questions. His answers seem like pulling teeth sometimes. By the time the sun sets, we are all ready for a movie and food night. Kylo asks for pizza and the guys seem to agree.

I wrap myself in a towel after putting on my dress cover. Grabbing the keys for the liquor closet that Stone didn't even return, I move towards everyone. I grab Stone's ass, making him glance over his shoulder at me. "Shower?"

He nods.

"Just got to return these to Silver. I'll meet you up there."

Stone nods, moving up the stairs in the foyer with all the other guys. Kira waits for me and when I move to Silver's office, she hangs in the living room.

Silver's door opens but it's Brick. "Hello, Ms. Esmeray."

"Hello, Brick. Just returning these bad boys," I say.

"Are you drunk and underage?" he teases, snatching the keys.

I scoff. "I had wine coolers. They are basically ice pops."

I hear Silver snort before speaking. "Esmeray, come in for a minute."

I glance back at Kira, and she gives me a shrug. I step inside. These two older men have looked out for me. They feel like fathers to me. So why am I nervous?

Rejected Wolf

Silver hands over a book. "It's hard to believe Reed made the connection before we did."

"So, he was right? You knew my dad. Were you guys' friends?"

He nods. "Packmates. Just look through that and if you have more questions, we can answer at another time."

My dad was a part of their pack...

I grab the book, clenching it. "Thank you... And that name that Reed said?"

He shrugs. "Don't worry about it, kid. It just was a guy we knew."

I nod. "Thanks." I move from the room, clenching the book before moving back out the living room.

Kira eyes the book. "What is it?"

"I don't know. My father's? Silver said to look through it before I ask any questions. I'm too scared to open it, but excited. But I want the pack there for it."

Kira touches my shoulder. "Go shower. We can open it after."

I nod, going up the stairs. We split off to the guest rooms. I open my door to see Stone's clothes on the floor and the shower water on. *Yeah, the book will have to wait.* I throw it on the bed after locking the door. I shed my wet clothes just as I see Zeno at the sink and Stone in the shower.

"Z," I acknowledge him.

His eyes run over my body. "I want to join."

260

I smile, biting my lip. I want nothing more than to fuck him in front of Stone. "Are you okay with that, Stone?"

The shower door opens. "It was my idea."

I reach forward, running a hand over Zeno's bare chest. "Then what are you waiting for? Get naked and get in." He chuckles. I move away, stepping in with Stone. I push his short brown hair back, ending with me grasping his jaw and pulling him to a kiss. He sweetly kisses me until he pulls me under the steaming water. There he kisses me feverishly, and nibbles on my lip a bit. Heat swirls inside of me as I grab his shoulders.

I feel Zeno behind me, kissing against my back, running his hands over my ass and hips.

Fuck. This is a sexy overload.

I run a hand down Stone's chest, down to his dick. I grab the shaft, leaning back to grab Zeno's. Both men are different, and I crave them both in the worst ways.

"Knees," Stone groans.

I drop to my knees and Stone guides me to his cock first as Zeno cleans himself a bit. I lick the tip, teasing his hole and tasting his salty precum. My pussy throbs as his dick twitches.

"No teasing," he orders.

I look up at him through my lashes, chuckling softly. "I'm not, Daddy." I push his tip into my mouth before sucking and swirling my tongue on it. He grabs

261

the back of my head and shoves himself into my mouth. I gag, closing my eyes.

"Play with me, Mami," Zeno says huskily.

My pussy throbs at the deep base of his voice, and I squeeze my thighs. My hand grabs his dick, rubbing it with the same pace as I suck Stone. I hallow my cheeks, falling into a rhythm. After a moment, I switch, taking Zeno's dick into my mouth and rubbing Stone.

I feel like a porn star. But more... realistic.

Zeno pushes himself into my throat, hissing. I've never sucked Zeno's dick. We just fucked a lot in one night. I take good care of him, using my tongue and swirling it around his shaft.

But Stone isn't having my softness, he pushes my head hard onto Zeno's dick. "Don't be afraid to hurt her. She likes it."

Fuck...

Zeno's fingers fist my hair, and he begins fucking my throat harshly. I squeeze my eyes shut, focusing on taking his dick without throwing up or gagging. "Fuck!" he groans.

A swirl of pleasure rushes through me.

Stone's hands grasp my hard nipple, and he pinches and rolls it.

I reach forward, grabbing Zeno's hips to steady my shaking body. I'm shaking with anticipation. I inhale, but it makes me gag and twitch. It makes him moan. Thick drool runs down my chin as he finally pulls away.

I breath out, moving to Stone. But before I can suck him, he pulls me to my feet. He bends me a bit to him. "Fuck her."

Zeno's hand spanks my ass hard, and with the water, it stings. I yelp, grabbing Stones chest.

"Shut up," Stone growls.

I smirk, feeling my legs shake. "Fuck me already!"

Zeno chuckles, spanking me again. He rubs the spot, fingers dipping lower touch my lips. His fingers spread them as he slid inside of me. His length enters so fucking easily. That's how wet I am.

I let out a sigh, looking up at Stone.

Stone's hand grasps my throat softly. "You want it?"

I nod as I try to move forward to get some relief.

"Beg for it. Beg for Zeno to fuck your pussy."

I close my eyes. "Don't make me."

Zeno slides out, but instead of thrusting back in. He pulls out fully.

"No! No!"

Stone's hands grasp my jaw to move me to face him. "Beg, baby."

My pussy throbs. I need a release from both of them or I might just die right here. "Please, fuck me Zeno."

Stone tsks. "What do you call him?"

I lick my lips. "Papi."

"Address him correctly next time"

"Fuck you," I say, feeling Zeno's finger brush my pussy. I twitch. "Just fuck me already, Papi. Please. I want to come so fucking bad!"

He slams into me and without warning, fucking me so hard and deep. Pleasure warms inside of me, making my body tingle. I cry out, grabbing Stone's cock and playing with it a bit. But he seems to be more focused on my face as his friend fucks me hard.

"Oh, fuck!" I moan, rubbing Stone faster. "Please don't stop!" I feel the heat waves of pleasure running through me. And when Stone's reaches down and plays with my clit, I literally sob. My pussy clench around Zeno, making his thrusts become harder.

My legs are shaking and although I am so close, I don't want it to end. I squeeze my eyes closed as Stone puts a finger into my mouth to suck. I suck on it, muffling my moans.

"I'm so close, Papi! Zeno! Zeno!" I cry out, pulling back, grabbing Stone's hips, and pushing hard onto Zeno. I clench, throwing my head back and shouting. The crash comes with a shudder. He slows his movement, ridding my high as I come undone on him and letting me moan it out.

"Shall we finish this outside the shower for a moment?" Zeno asks, but I doubt he's talking to me.

My body is shaking like jelly, and I can't think straight yet.

Stone scoops me up, carrying me out of the shower. He doesn't take me far, setting me down on my knees. Zeno moves in front of me against the counter. I look up, seeing him smirking down at me. Stone sits down below me, putting his legs under mine and lifting me so I'm doing reverse cowgirl on him.

Dear god. The shit that he comes up with.

Stone grabs my hips and pulls me down against him. I gasp, but he enters me easily with a slight groan. I reach up, touching Zeno's hard shaft. Veins line his dick to his tip and his balls are tight. He's so close to coming.

I lick his tip, moaning and rising from Stone's dick. Soon, I follow in a fast rhythm of bouncing and sucking hard on Zeno. Zeno grunts, letting me do my own thing and not choking me as much.

Stone lifts his knees, pulling me close. His finger finds my clit when he reaches around me, making me pull back and moan. "Please!" I don't even know what I'm begging for, yet here I am begging.

We all fall in a rhythm, leaving my legs shaking and my moans loud. Heat has washed over me, and the familiar pressure of an orgasm is starting.

"Please, don't stop! Please, don't stop!" I cry over and over like I knew what I was begging for. I want to come so badly. Zeno grabs my head and makes me suck him hard as Stone bounces his hips hard, thrusting inside of me. Pleasure tightens and ripples through me. I grip Zeno's hips, digging my fingers into it. Stone doesn't let up on my clit as he begins to moan. He's close. I tighten around him. It sends me over the edge, but I can't cry out. Instead, my body twitches and slows with the muffled moans. Stone and Zeno don't stop.

Zeno's fist tightens in my hair, slamming my face onto his cock. Then his cock twitches, and he's coming down my throat. Some drips out of my mouth and down my chin onto the floor. He pulls back, groaning.

I swallow and let out a soft whimper. My body straight as I bounce with Stone until finally he digs his fingers in my hips, slamming into me and moaning loudly. I tighten around him, milking him and letting his cum seep out of me.

Esmeray

I throw my damp curls up into a ponytail as I sit in the living room. Kira hands over a beer, in her little pj's. I'm matching her, but in black and white. Both shorts with crop tank tops. I try not to make eye contact with the new twins. I feel like in a way, they know that I really did have sex with four guys today.

"Took you long enough. Order the food already," Krew mutters. I sip my drink, throwing the blue book at him. He groans. "What's this?"

I chug the beer, then breathe. I'm nervous, I'm not even sure what might be in there. "Silver said my dad was a part of his pack."

Kai grabs the book, eyeing it. "Looks like a picture book."

I push Kai's legs apart, sitting on the ground between his legs. He hands over the book. "I figured you guys can be here when I open it." Nerves run through me. *Maybe I shouldn't open it. Maybe something bad happened with this Dan guy.* I bit my lip.

Zeno sits in front of me, touching my knee. "You want to know, right?"

"No," I say, biting my lip.

Xave snorts. "I would. It's nothing to be nervous about."

How can he tell I'm nervous? "I'm as cool as a cucumber."

Kylo lets out a laugh. "Normally, people who say that are not okay."

I roll my eyes. "Apparently everyone is smart now, huh?" I rub the book before opening it. Stone sits next to me, and I can feel Kylo peering over Kai's shoulder. Xave might not care much.

I swallow at the first picture. It's a picture of my father with Stone's, Krew and Kai's, and Zeno's father. Arm in arm. Reed's father is off to the side talking to an Asian guy.

"That's our dad," Kylo mutters.

Xave shifts behind us, moving closer. "Huh?"

"So, my dad is here." I brush my fingers over the guy. Then over the date and the title. "The pack."

268

Suddenly my chest aches. Silver knew my father, and here I am. Fate has brought us all together. They have brought me back to my pack. The pack my father had as well. "Then... Silver, Krew's and Kai's, Zeno's and then Redmen."

Kylo points to the Asian man. "That's our dad."

"This is crazy..." Kai mutters.

I flip the page to see my father on a bike. He holds his helmet with a huge smile on his face. I recognize the bike. "That's Ruby, dad's first bike... He talked about it non-stop. He crashed it one night when I was eleven... and it was his worst day ever." I chuckle at the memory, eyes tearing up.

"You guys look alike," Stone mutters, kissing my head.

I bounce a brow. "He said I looked like my mother. He said my mom made jokes that she hopes I didn't get his looks because he had huge ears."

Krew moves my hair behind my ear. "Is that why you have long hair?"

I hit his hand away. "Stop it."

He smiles, turning the page. The next picture is my father with me in his arms, and I'm a baby, bundled up. His eyes are bright and twinkling as he looks down at me. He used to tell me he wanted nothing more than to be a father. He knew that's what he wanted when everyone else wanted to be something else when they got older. He just wanted to be my dad.

My dad. No one else's. My eyes start to tear up again. He looks at me like I was the best thing in the fucking world.

Clearing my throat, I flip the page. This picture is of Silver and my father. They have each other in headlocks and are seemingly laughing.

Stone bumps me.

I smile. "Do you think they were best friends?"

He shrugs. "Probably, if Dad had this book."

I flip the page, and this is with Silver and Liza with my father and a Spanish woman.

"Is that your mom?" Krew asks.

I shake my head. "No. Dad said she was white. My dad was African and Cuban, so... I doubt she's my mother. But he said he never had a mate. He was always a lone wolf in that sense."

"Is that possible? Everyone has a pack, and everyone has a mate, right?" Zeno asks, looking at Kai, of course, for the answer.

Kai shakes his head, making me look up. "Sometimes wolves don't."

"I'm not sure if my dad was in this pack. He would have lived closer, right?"

Kai shrugs. "Most of the time they do live nearby just in case they are needed. I'm not sure why he lived so far or why Kylo's and Xave's parents lived even further."

Rune Hunt

I turn the page and see a picture of just Kylo's and Xave's dad and mom. Xave inhales, moving away. I look to Kylo. "What's your dad's name?"

He smiles sadly. "Kane. Kane and Lily were our parents." His eyes are on the picture. I remove the picture from the plastic slot and hand it over. Our eyes meet as he hesitates to take it. "Thanks…"

I nod. I turn back to the book and flip through it and see all the pictures that make me smile. The last picture is like the one I have. It's of me; a chubby two-year-old with my rune on my back but I was facing my father, moving to him. His look is of pure fucking joy.

My eyes sting with tears again, but this time, they run down my face.

I hate thinking about how happy we were before his death. I hate thinking that he'll never be around to see me grow up or have kids or even walk me down the aisle when I get married. He never got to experience the best things in having children. He raised me, stepped up when my mom left. And he wasn't even here. *How unfair is that?*

Stone pulls me against his chest. "Don't cry, Esmeray."

My palms dry my eyes before tears can fall. "My dad… had never wanted anything more than to be my dad, and he wasn't perfect. We struggled but it never felt like struggling because… he made it work…"

Krew touches my shoulder. "How do you think he'd react to you having all these mates?"

Rejected Wolf

I snort. "Fight every single one of you. He thought no one would ever be good enough. But…" I sniff. "He would come to like you guys and decide you guys were good enough for me."

Stone kisses my forehead.

The picture shifts in the sleeve as I sit back up. "Sorry, I'm a cry baby." But something behind the photo catches my eye. I reach behind it and pull it out.

It's a note with my name written on it.

"What is that?" Zeno questions.

"It's my dad's handwriting." I take a deep breath before opening it and begin reading out loud. "*Little moon*," I smile at his nickname. No nickname will ever beat this. "*If you're ever reading this, that means two things; you've met Silver. Isn't he such a pain in the ass?*" I smile. "*Two, you might be ready to realize something we've hid from you.*" My smile fades, but I continue reading aloud. "*You might know by now that you're a shifter. If not, surprise! Your pops is a wolf and so are you. Moon, I knew the risks in hiding this from you. I also knew the risks in having Claire take… your memories away.*"

"What?" Kai says.

I sit up on my knees. "*Something happened, Moon, and I was unable to be the parent you needed at that time. At eleven, you were forced to have your first shift. The doctors all said that you might not have a shift again for a while because of that, and the memories Claire took from you.*"

272

Rune Hunt

Little moon, it's time to remember. Remember the first time you shifted. The voice from the dream is eerily on point now.

"I had her take them, so don't be too mad. What?!" I shoot my feet, moving from the living room. I hear my pack behind me, coming in just as hot as I am. I find the adults in the dining room, drinking whiskey. "What?!" I look at Claire wide eyed. "*What* did you do?"

She stays silent, looking at me.

I repeat what I read in the letter. "*At eleven, you were forced to have your first shift. The doctors all said that you might not have a shift again for a while because of that and the memories Claire took from you. I had her take them so don't be too mad.*" I throw down the letter and book. "What memories did you take?"

Silence.

"Were they of my mother?"

She shakes her head. "Something bad... happened."

My skin crawls as blood rushes from my face.

"You shifted to protect yourself. Your father didn't think you should remember."

I throw my hands up. "Is this stopping me from shifting?" I look at Silver who look down at his drink then back at Claire.

She nods. "Sometimes your memories being taken away will... block chakras. In this case, it blocked a few. It blocked your Sahasrara: the crown, your vishuddha: the throat, and maybe your svadhishthana: the sacral. Wolves thrive on having all their chakra being aligned to shift. Yours are off…"

"So, fix it."

She looks down. "Child, that involves giving back horrific memories."

My mouth clamps closed. Where they really that bad? What happened? "Why were they taken in the first place?"

"You couldn't cope with what happened, Esmeray. You... just…" Silver struggles to say.

"How many children do you know named Esmeray?" I snap. "How did you not know it was me?"

"It's actually common," Brick says. "Everyone wants to be named something with the moon. If we give the memories back... you'll relive it."

I let out a huff. "So, I might not be able to shift because you guys don't want to give me back my memories. They are mine! If I don't shift, no one goes back to the academy."

Stone touches my hip. "It doesn't matter if we don't go back."

I let out a sigh. "I have to learn how to protect us from the Oni wolves. They are obviously after us because of me. We have so much to learn and do. I need to know how to protect you guys from almost dying."

Stone scans my face, pulling my face to his. "If you want to do this, you will relive the traumatic thing in your life."

Anger rises in my throat. "Is it worse than watching your dad take his last breath? Or your mate with a tube down his fucking throat? Don't you want to know what they are hiding from us?"

He licks his lips and shakes his head. "Honestly... No. I don't like seeing you unhappy. But if you need to know... I will support anything you want to do. We all will, baby."

"I might not ever shift into a wolf... Isn't that... sad?"

He shrugs. "We know you're a shifter. You will still be our mate and our alpha."

I shake my head, moving his hands away from me. "It's... not the same. You guys grew up wanting to be in this academy. I know it crushed you to have it closed..."

He closes his lips, but nods.

"Are you sure about this?" Claire asks.

"I need to know. My dad felt like he needed to protect me from it. But I'm not a kid anymore." I glance at Kai and Krew. Krew gives me a soft smile. Zeno touches my hip, nodding.

I even look to Kylo, who says, "You have your pack behind you."

"Can you do it, Claire?" Zeno asks. "Give her back her memories?"

Claire nods.

"What if… it's really bad?" Kai asks, chewing on his inner cheek. "What if it destroys you?"

I look down at the note. I've been through the toughest things in my life. I lost my mother, my father, my childhood best friend to the fire, and I almost lost my mates. I need to be able to protect them and by being a wolf… I can protect them.

My father had no right playing with my memories.

Claire stands. "Okay, child. If this is truly what you want, let's move to the living room."

Esmeray

Nerves run down my spine and through my bone. I am not changing my mind, but I just think about what it could be. *If it's bad, will my mates leave me? Would they reject me like Reed did?*

Stone sends a wave of positivity down our bond, letting me know he's behind me. I feel more of what they feel, and I know they all support me, even if I murdered someone. Krew said that to me, making me smile before. Even Kylo and Xave have gotten along with everyone, like we've always been friends. They seem to be standing by my side.

Rejected Wolf

I swallow hard as Claire sits in front of me. "Are you positive?"

"How bad is it, Claire?" I whisper.

She sighs. "You seem to have a good pack and support system."

"Can you at least tell me what happened?" I ask.

She swallows. "It's hard to say. Are you ready?"

I nod. *Ready as I'll ever be.*

Claire rolls her shoulders, muttering a chant. At this point it isn't too bad to assume Claire is a witch and a wolf. I sit and watch her; her eyes roll back until they are pure white. *Okay, creepy.* Claire finally reaches out and touches my head.

Goosebumps rise against my skin as all my hair stands up. I inhale sharply before a flood of information enters my head like a freight train.

Images of blood covering my skin and my clothing. *So much blood.*

My body aches and parts of my skin are cut up. I look at my hands, seeing blood and shredded skin under my nails. My eyes move lower down my body. Blood runs down between my legs.

"It's okay, little moon. I protected you." *The same voice that wanted me to remember says that.* "I protected my Goddess."

Twisting, I look down and see it.

Rune Hunt

A body lying in the middle of the floor. A gasp catches in my throat. His skin has been torn to shreds, his chest is leaking blood all over the carpet. My wide eyes move up to his face until I realize... He has no face. Claws marks have made his face unrecognizable.

A scream catches in my throat, turning away from it.

Hands grabs me and I scream even fucking louder until I realize it's Stone. I look at him with soaked eyes and cheeks. *When was I crying? Why...? The body...* My hands are shaking as I finally break. Tears rush down my face as I let out a sob.

"What happened?" Stone's brows pull together.

"I—" I hiccup.

He reaches for me again, but when I flinch, he freezes. "Esmeray?"

"Breathe, baby," Kai mutters to me.

I inhale sharply, swallowing. It takes me a moment to even calm the shaking sobs in my body. "I... I killed him, Stone. I didn't... I didn't mean to... I—"

He blinks. "Es—"

"My father..." I swallow, feeling so many eyes burning on me. I need to explain before they leave me. But the words are so fucking hard. Tears rush down my face as I quickly say, "It was a routine. I get home at three-twenty. I was eleven, but I knew... I knew how to cook. Dad would be home at four-thirty. So I

279

cooked, and I cleaned. That was my routine. Cl-clean and co-cook. We've had this routine for a while."

"Esmeray…?" I freeze, hearing Kai's soft voice. "Slow down, baby. Tell us what happened."

"He… He was getting home at seven that day. Meeting. I forgot. I cooked so much food… We had neighbors in that apartment building. They fought all the time but the woman… she… was nice. I went over. I gave them food, explained that my dad wasn't going to be home in time and that there—there were extras."

I meet Stone's eyes, bearing into the bright blue eyes.

"I was being nice! After I cleaned the kitchen up, someone knocked… The husband was returning the dishes and making sure I didn't need anything. I…" Tears roll down my face. "I thought he was being nice. I thought he…" I take a deep shaky breath before going into a numbing calm. I swallow as pins and needles run along my body, raising hair against my skin. My eyes move to the floor in front of me. "He pulled a knife on me. He was so much bigger than I was."

"Esmeray. You don't have to tell us," Stone says, hand shaking as if he knew what was going to happen.

But I am numb… It doesn't hurt anymore… "He overpowered me quickly, putting the knife to my throat. Said if I screamed, he would kill me and then my father when he got back. He said that he would

280

keep him alive long enough to just cry and realize that I was gone. He said he did this so often that all the little girls listened each time."

"Fuck!" Krew mutters, voice shaking. I hear him shuffle behind me.

"So, I stayed quiet as he ripped off my clothes. Then I froze…" I look up at Stone, sucking on my salty bottom lip. "He raped me, and I froze. I didn't move an inch since he had cut me each time that I did."

Stone's eyes grow wet and his breathing changes heavily.

"I was pissed. *At myself.* How could I let that happen? Dad taught me everything I needed to know, and I did nothing. I didn't scream to get help. The walls were fucking thin. I didn't dial 911 or dad's number. I didn't do anything."

"You were a kid," Kylo's shaking voice comes.

"I blacked out and when I came to, he was dead. Torn to shreds by my wolf. I didn't feel… *bad.* I didn't care that I killed him. I called Dad and told him what happened. I passed out by the time he got home."

Silver steps forward, clearing his throat. "Your dad called us. Redman, Brick, and Kane. We came just as quick as he did. But he didn't tell us everything. We found you cuddled with a blanket in the closet, and that sight was worse than the body."

Rejected Wolf

I lick my lips, looking at my pack. Zeno's fists were so tight, they looked like they might bleed. Krew is pacing, hands in hair. Kai is kneeling beside me, wanting to touch me. Stone is in front of me, hand running over his face. Kylo is sitting, face in hands. Xave is the only one I can't read. Our eyes meet.

"I know I just met you…" Xave starts. "But I'm glad you killed him because none of the men in your life—including me—would have let that fucker live."

My bottom lip quivers and tears rush down my face again. I call down my bond for someone to touch me or hug me.

Stone is the first to react, scooping me up in his arms. I bury my face in his neck, sobbing. My shoulders shake with each sob.

"What did you do with the body?" Zeno questions.

Brick sighs. "Redmen wanted to call the cops, but we knew we couldn't. A shifter killed him. Kane and Silver took Esmeray to the hospital, although she healed pretty quickly after shifting. Ernie took the fall with the council. He said he came home and saw him… and killed him in a rage. Ernie was outcasted."

I pull back. "Is that why we lived so far away?"

Silver nods. "Yes. I wanted him to just let me get rid of the body, so he could stay, but he couldn't do that to our pack… but after a straight month of nightmares and not eating, he brought you back one night and that's when Claire erased your memories."

"I don't remember you... You guys."

"Your dad lived far away to begin with. He worked all the time, and we had kids too. It just never worked out. But I would go back in time to at least offer to check in that day. And I know, E would have never stayed late if he knew. He felt like he failed you."

I shake my head, letting Kai wipe away my tears. "It wasn't his fault... Silver, how is it possible I shifted so early?"

"Your wolf was protecting you or trying to," Claire starts. "She got brought up by the rage you felt."

"Rage. And that is what she thrives off of now. When that twenty-one-year-old came at me with a knife, I freaked out I guess and beat her up. Probably reminded me of when..."

Yeah. Enough said.

Kira touches my shoulder. I twist to see her. She's been crying. When I see that, it makes me start crying again. She presses her forehead against mine. "You are so strong, even at eleven, Esmeray."

I don't feel strong. I feel broken and beaten. But I also felt enlightened. I remembered the first time I shifted. I remember what I looked like.

Black fur covered in white spots like the ones I have on my skin. Blood dripping as I looked up at myself in the mirror. Then I saw her in the mirror, standing over me, petting me and soothing me. She wasn't there in reality. I knew I could only see her. Her hair was white and long, shimmering under every light. Her eyes were a pale white, dark bronze skin in the similar spots as mine. A small smirk on her face when she said, "*It's okay, little moon. My wolf, Luna, will protect you. You are, and forever will be, the Goddess Luna reincarnated.*"

Stone

I wait until I hear the bedroom door close to speak. Zeno has taken Esmeray upstairs. "*Fuck.*" I want to hit something, break something. I would never let anything hurt my girl.

My father touches my shoulder. "Stone. There's something you need to know…"

What more? What else can there be? I glance at Brick and Xave.

"Redmen called the council on Ernie and Esmeray. They know she shifted and what she did. But they let E take the fall."

"What?!" My brows pull together.

He lets out a huff. "It was really hard to trust Redman after what he did. We all got in a lot of trouble, including Kane who was outcasted as well for help."

That sounds oddly familiar. "So, why are we friends with him and his kid?"

"Because you keep your friends close… but your enemies even closer."

All the information is too much to take in, but with a nod, I move away. My mate needs me now more than ever.

When I get upstairs, I look at Esmeray bundled up in blankets surrounded by mattresses on the floor. Zeno cuddles her, muttering positive things in her ear. She looks up at us with wet eyes.

Fuck. I wish for someone to touch her again. I would be the one covered in blood. I would kill anyone for her.

The End of Book Two

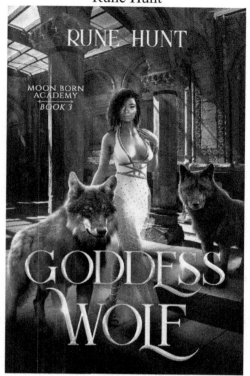

RUNE HUNT

MOON BORN
ACADEMY
BOOK 3

GODDESS
WOLF

I remember who I am
And It's the first female Alpha and Goddess Luna.
Time is running out for my small pack that keeps
getting bigger by the day. After finally getting my
suppressed memories back from Claire, I have a little
over a month to shift to be able to return to Moon Born
Academy.
But there are demonic wolves called oni wolves after
us. With little time to shift into a wolf and oni wolves
always around, my pack is in for trouble.

More from the Author

—The Blood Artifact Trilogy—
Blood and Snow
Bloodline
Blood Artifact

—Preorders—
Hell's Reaper—a hellhound shifter and grim reaper
academy romance
Insatiable—a monster romance novella

Follow my social medias for more updates.
Facebook—Rune Hunt
Facebook Group—Rune Hunt's Reverse Harem
Tiktok—Authornotsafeforwarfare

Printed in Great Britain
by Amazon